Gateway into Mayhem

Liam Adams

Cover illustration by Liam Adams

Gateway into Mayhem

by Liam Adams

everyoneneedsaliam.com.au

We think this book is mostly suited to children from 10 years old, and young adults, 12 and over, although older adults may enjoy it as much!

This book is copyright and may not be reproduced in any manner without consulting the author. All intellectual property including cover artwork belongs to the author.

This book is sold on the understanding that it is the work of a person with intellectual disability and Autism. All creativity is from the author and the text has been edited by his mother to the best of her ability. However, it is understood that the writing may be different from that expected in a formally published novel.

Liam hopes you enjoy reading his book as much as he enjoyed writing it. He would love to hear your feedback; if you wish to contact him his email address is
ltahm@icloud.com

Canberra, Australia

May, 2024

ISBN: 978-0-6455970-5-9

Table of Contents

Preface

Why hello again! Just came back after avoiding oblivion in space by a ton of alien ships. I haven't any idea what got under their skin, but I think they may want copies of this newest book. So, I think you must be ready for the next chapter of the Librarian Saga: Gateway into Mayhem!

Without getting too distracted, I should tell you about the progress of this dazzling and quite unexpected novel.

It really does live up to the title. This was one where I knew the main thing when you become a storyteller is to tell a story…but this book takes you through a lot of twisted turns.

We've seen stuff already in the librarian saga about world building - there's a system where humanity is kept prisoner, and another where it's all related to a dying tree - but here, you go to so many places and then discover rich and unknown history. But the exiting thing is, you'll get a lot more of that here than you're expecting.

There isn't really a thread of a story here. I just wanted Floyd to tag along with a group of people he just met who are just seeking an adventure across the galaxy. That's it, nothing more to it.

But wherever they go, there are small story plot points in every few chapters. It nearly feels like you're getting a collection of few misadventure stories in one book.

They get in trouble a lot of the time, but sometimes they just find somewhere where they can finally relax. You get enough time as these little stories arc throughout the book and I just loved that.

I had better describe Gateway into Mayhem as a bit of Improv drama. Floyd and the Mercent Siblings are the Improvers (just as I have done Improv drama in real life). They do act out, as I imagine anyone would, giving silly attention to the situation they are in and just being themselves while trying to get out of it.

But I should talk about the Mercent Siblings, shouldn't I? Yeah, they're being possibly the most exiting bunch of characters I've written for our librarian to team up with.

You get Benny (of course I have to talk about Benny first), who I imagine as the gentle kind soul he is. For most parts of the book, he seems like an adopted brother of Floyd. He is quite bubbly and he just wants to play Sa-Booth, the greatest game of all time! Who wouldn't want to play Sa-Booth with this guy?

Then we get Lilly, who I made to be the up-front leader who knows her brother Alex isn't good at leading. She has skills and advantages that help the crew out of many scenarios. She also has good moments as she's quite likable but also keeps everyone focussed.

And Alex - which to be honest, I like writing Alex. He is sneezy and quite one-minded, but that's all he is really. A hippy who's a bit of a buzz kill and seems to isolate himself from any other activities around him; but yet again, that's what he is.

The original concept I had with this book when I was brainstorming it was that I wanted a book (almost with the same story as this), where Floyd is accompanied by three strangers. I think some of my earlier drafts were that they were isolated on a planet for a couple of years, and suddenly Floyd was there and there they go, setting off into some misadventures.

The Mercent Siblings were originally meant to be some blokes, or dudes, but I changed few of the ideas around when I designed the Mercent Siblings, so they can be more fleshed out and be, well, new and unexpected.

I did notice that the term 'Mayhem' does get referenced a lot in the book. Parts of it I didn't mean to leave in there, but to the theming of the book, I think it just sticks well. Because that's really the point of Gateway into Mayhem - its Floyd and the Mercent Siblings getting into as much mayhem as they can.

I wrote this straight after I did my first draft of System of Trees, and what a plan! Another amazing addition to the Librarian Saga series!

I hope you'll have both a joy and a blast reading it, as it has been for me. Better prepare yourself for the unexpected, the wild, and what awaits on the other side!

Liam Adams, Summer 2024

1. We'll See You in Doom!

In the Sta System lay the 'planet of hell' - there wasn't any better name anyone could come up with than that. A prison planet, you could call it. It was a desert world with ranges of tall rocky mountains with prisons shaped inside them, and each mountain a mile apart from another.

It was boiling with heat and pain; mountains exploded once in a while as they turned into bursting volcanos. Fallen rocks flew out of the volcanos or sometimes through the planet's hypersphere.

Prisoners were complaining in cells through bars in the mountains. Sometimes they got dragged out to do some jobs by the unsocialized creatures known as the Ban. The Ban ruled this world, keeping every eye on their guests and making their lives a living pain.

There was no guarantee of safety on the planet. Either you would die in the heat in the worst conditions, get hunted down or killed by the Ban, or get exploded by any of the prison mountains you were in. You just had to put your own life in fate's hands.

Mau Heck, Captain of the planet Tasha and the Bans, made his way to visit one of the prisoners. The prisoner was in a cave-like room where he was in a machine that glowed red and was steaming. It was all made of bricks and bars with a small window on each side.

The prisoner was a funny addition that Mau thought of. Everyone was human or some other species, who didn't have rough and rusty grey skin like the Ban. And still, this prisoner wore peculiar clothes.

The prisoner was none other than Floyd. You know? Librarian? Last living thing of existence? Who carried the responsibility of guarding a library that drifted into the blackness of nothingness at the end of time?

Well, he was meant to travel to a luxury world of Bib Bobs in the Ixia system, but he accidentally dropped out of the ship he was in and arrived here. He didn't really have any plans to visit Tasha. He knew that this entire sector in the galaxy was pretty much dangerous, and he tried to avoid it as much as possible.

He spent days on this planet, and he met many locals: ones that helped him and then tried to kill him. And he also met Mau Heck, and they got along well (Not!).

Mau Heck caught Floyd trying to make an escape plan with the other prisoners. But that failed as everyone else had eyes on them and no one was keeping quiet. But something kept Mau Heck questioning this man, and the only way to do so was to break him.

Floyd was kept at one of the higher levels of the mountains where he could hear screams and evil laughter; this was basically normal on Tasha.

The machine Floyd was in was steaming with heat inside and drew him into a worse condition. Floyd knew that this world made heat to make everyone suffer.

"Boy," Floyd said, in a sweat. He could handle many impossible challenges; this wasn't doing the trick. "I could get through this if you put more heat in this thing! But no more than that!"

Mau Heck laughed simultaneously as he wandered around Floyd, seeing how far Floyd's plan came to fail and that he had no escape. "How do you like my heat machine?" the captain joked.

Floyd laughed with him, as his face kept sweating dimly. "Ah, I see what you did there. Heat? Machine? You sure have a sense of humour."

Mau clanged closer to one of the bars where he could make eye contact with Floyd. "There's no escape," he warned, as he knew the chance of that happening was extremely unlikely. "You are mine, and you shall surrender all your plans to me!"

"If I want to," Floyd responded, as he turned his head away from the captain. "You know, I could do this for another week, or maybe two weeks and an episode of whatever TV show is on."

Mau blew his nose as he showed a face of aggression. He was trying to pin out the information that the librarian was holding. "I have seen your cleverness. How easy it was for you and the other prisoners to get out. You can't hide what you are planning."

"That's why I'm not saying anything." Floyd tried to get his attention away from Mau. Floyd knew what he was doing would work eventually, but he knew there was no easy ticket out of this.

"Everyone has wanted to get out of that thing for years," Mau told Floyd. "There will not be any easy tricks in there."

"Listen, I left my robots to do their jobs, a teenage boy is focusing on his homework or chilling out with his friends on a space station, and a girl from the past has better things to do than to be in this ditch. I have no plan!" Floyd exclaimed.

"Ahhh! You can't fool me!" Mau said as he clanged much closer to the bar. He could feel the tension that something was going on. "You may think you have enough time tormenting yourself in here, but you know deep down that there is something you are hiding."

"You know what?" Floyd told the captain, opening up. "As you are very curious about this whole thing, I might tell you something…"

"and what's that?"

Meanwhile, inside the machine, Floyd was fiddling with some wires through the pipes underneath. The machine was a seat so he couldn't move or see what he was doing, but he could tell what his hands were fiddling with and that was giving him clues.

The librarian scanned his fingers to find what was the right wire to pull. He could tell it could be either of these options: a green wire, a purple wire, or a red wire.

"Hmmm…." he thought. "This might take some time."

He pulled one of the wires as the steaming machine blew like a train and the machine's door flew straight onto Mau, which got him flying. When Floyd got out of it, he noticed Mau had crashed into the wall and was unconscious. But Floyd knew he would wake up at some point, which got Floyd moving, and fast!

Floyd went outside to stand on the wooden planks. He could see he was in a high view of the planet, and everything below seemed like a world of nightmare. The sky was full of brown clouds in a dead environment; the suns were bright enough to be noticed, and the mountains you could see were not that far apart.

Wooden planks were carving all around the mountains. A bunch of Bans were roaming and shouting orders at their prisoners, while levers were pulling many types of objects to different levels. There was also a point where the Ban's ships parked on a smooth surface of the mountain.

Floyd was walking about stealthily until he could hear Mau's men yelling at the prisoners and footsteps coming in Floyd's direction. He crept over to an archway to watch them move along. The archway was cramped, and Floyd knew it wasn't really a good hiding spot: he could be spotted any moment. Luckily from Floyd's perspective, no one spotted him yet.

All the prisoners wore raggy clothes with their hair so long, while the Ban wore scraps of metal that gave a sense of how dangerous this place was.

There was a long line-up until the last scouts marched behind the last prisoners and then the noises became quiet. Floyd took a moment to breathe as he checked the coast was clear and then he dashed out of the area.

Floyd knew that trying to escape was impossible; trying to escape the planet was also very unlikely. Floyd also knew that Mau was another problem. That meant that to get out of here, Floyd wouldn't get a chance like this ever again.

Floyd ran as he didn't have time for hide and seek. He never liked that game, but he knew he couldn't play it out here. Shortly after, the scouts noticed him running, which caused an alarm.

"Hey! Prisoner on the loose!"

Floyd heard many angry scouts, as every time he turned around, they were either behind or above him.

Floyd sprinted as he needed to use all the energy he had. He climbed up ladders, jumped on platforms that had been pulled by an elevator and took him to different levels. But Floyd also noticed that every time he got further away, he got more of a crowded attention which lured multiple Bans.

These aliens didn't have weapons on them, or they should have thought of them in the first place. When they saw Floyd escaping, they had nothing to do but to yell out their lungs.

Floyd climbed up a ladder as he noticed many Bans were on his trail. What the Librarian did next was to kick it over as the Bans were holding on tight. It made a crash landing on the nearest plank with a heavy thud.

Floyd kept making his way, passing through cave-like tunnels where he saw some of the prisoners working, some that had betrayed him on their previous escape.

Floyd made a few turns across different pathways, hoping they were ones that the Bans wouldn't find him in. But that wasn't the case as about seven Bans were walking in his direction and spotted the Librarian. Floyd froze then turned around as he headed to another tunnel which led him back outside.

He kept running down a long plank until he noticed that their flying crafts from below drifted over to his level and hovered. They had two spiralling wing turbines that looked like gold helicopters in a way.

Floyd had other diversions as he jumped on the edge of a plank and grabbed a rope that swung up through a connected platform. Floyd climbed up on the rope while basically everyone watched him. They were stunned and amazed that someone not very athletic could do something so talented as this.

The platform moved him around the mountain as the Bans tried to reach him, but it took a different turn. It went up and Floyd sped up many levels ahead of them, leading him to his next action in the plan.

When it stopped, the level Floyd was on led him to a cave which no one was in. He was left with only a couple of seconds, at best, to block off the entrance and barricade himself. Floyd had one last piece of his escape plan which would blow that rock! Literally!

He had sent a message to someone he knew. It took him about a few days to send that message while being trapped inside the heat machine. But the sending of the message lagged on this world, so Floyd had to time it perfectly.

The message said, 'Pick me up.' Nothing more.

Floyd's outrageous plan was that his pickup would pick him up as the mountain he was in exploded. He needed to be in the right spot at a safe distance to fly out and head towards his pickup.

The cave had a computer system that had buttons and wires, which Floyd fiddled and flicked about. The guards and scouts were trying to get him out as there was a shield bar door that stopped them getting in.

As much as it was ridiculous, Floyd was proud of his plan. He wasn't sure if it would work or would get him killed, but he thought it might have to do.

While Floyd continued his work, a familiar figure came to the door which posed a terminating threat.

"U!@!" roared out Mau Heck, who cut through his men in line. "If you dare think of doing something so despicable…"

"What?" Floyd asked, while trying to not listen but focussing on flicking the controls. "I thought you were going to warn me about the mountain exploding?"

Floyd glared at Mau, which for the first time kept him quiet. "I know exactly when the exploding will happen, which will be in the next couple of seconds."

"You won't get away from me that easily!" Mau clanged his head into the bar as his men ran. He had never had a loose prisoner in all of his career, and he wasn't going to let one go free now.

"Why do you think I'm in here?" Floyd told the captain, as if he was speaking to the captain as a fool. "I'm like three steps ahead of you now. There's little chance of succeeding now if you would let this one go and…"

Floyd paused as he faced the shaping colours in the room, which brightened red as the buttons flashed and the screen showed high levels of radiation.

"Oh," Floyd spoke softly, "you should really take your men out of the mountain and pull them back."

"What about you?" Mai asked, as he knew it would mean Floyd would die in the process.

"Easy piny disy…" Floyd commented, then stopped and froze as he rethought his plan. He only had a couple of chances for this to really work, but it raised some dry and dim issues which he never focussed on properly.

Mau left him to die as he ran for shelter. Floyd looked down at all his progress as if he really didn't think this through.

"Wait!" he said to himself. "Maybe this was a bad idea!"

Before he could rush towards the locked door, the controls started to flare and the next thing Floyd knew, he was blown away, flying in ash and booming around the mountain. Lava curled from within the mountain as it slid down towards the surface.

Mau did call back his men and brought the prisoners just in time before the mountain exploded. They were in their nearest transport when they saw the mountain blowing up.

Floyd flew in slow motion; he flew hundreds and even thousands of feet high above where he could see everything. He thought in a strange moment that he may never think this mayhem would end.

For the first time since he abandoned his post at the Library, he just wanted to go home. No more hollows, no more robots, no more lizards with big guns, no plant monsters, or even bizarre-looking creatures. He just wanted to settle in. Floyd wasn't really an unadventurous type, but he knew how it felt when you had too much on your plate.

Not so far away, as Floyd finished daydreaming, he was diving down and about to crash into another mountain, where lay more of Mau's men. Even Floyd thought he had had about enough of staying on this planet.

But Floyd's hope came: a spaceship called the Olivas drifted on its side as Floyd flew right into it. When Floyd crash landed on the metal floor, the Olivas drifted up into the sky and blasted out of obit.

Floyd collapsed on the floor, as the ship's hall was like an air force aeroplane's room where army troops sat on either side. But this was no rescue squad. As Floyd looked up it was his old friend Nile (who wore different clothes) who he knew Floyd was in need of help.

"How have you been, Floyd?" Nile asked the Librarian, as it had been some time they had seen each other. Like, five years ago. Maybe six years ago.

Floyd was breathing hard as he tried to either dry out the ash or he was in distress. His heart was bouncing in the wrong way than before, and his sweat shallowed like he was melting in an ice cream machine.

"No more!" Floyd called, as he got up on his own and walked over to the pilot room where he met another old friend he hadn't seen in a long time - Gammon.

"Oh, hi Floyd!" Gammon greeted him.

Floyd ignored the greeting as his brain functions couldn't work anymore. It was driving him so that Floyd couldn't tell how to relax.

"No, no", Floyd complained, "I am not doing another adventure like that again! Not another one! No more!"

"You don't really mean that." Nile commented as he entered the room and put a smile on the librarian.

"No, not really," Floyd agreed, as no one would argue with that. He sat on the next passenger seat which was like a gamer's chair design. He moped as he tried to for the moment to chill down. "But I really need to lay low somewhere for a little while. Maybe a few weeks at least."

"Hmm," Nile commented, as he scrolled on his small device from the Talen System. He tried to research habitable planets nearby. "You sure have a way of getting yourself around. The Sta System isn't really a place you really want to make yourself at home."

"You should go to Levith," Gammon suggested, "I've heard it's nice, beautiful oceans…"

"I'm not sure Floyd really means something that low, Gammon." Nile told him. Nile had no idea why he recruited him in the first place; he knew somebody suggested that he should be involved in a major operation but now Nile just couldn't get rid of him. "Any ideas, Floyd?"

"I don't know," Floyd sighed as no ideas came to mind, "to the same old."

"All right," Nile said, as he nodded to Gammon, and the Oliva headed into their next destination.

2.   A Band of Troubling Siblings

Lightyears away through the cosmos lay Osram Stars: a galaxy-connected space station where those from every sector across the galaxy came to visit. It wasn't originally meant to be built on its popularity, but they had little choice when it came to be on the list of top five best space stations.

It was full of wonders of colour on every single level. It felt like you were going to a proper town with different shops from different parts of the galaxy. They also had a range of activities that any visitor could choose.

Alien locals came here once in a while, including new ones who just randomly found their way here. Everyone fancied Osram Stars as it was their beacon through the galaxy, and they knew it was the one place to have a pit stop whenever they went on their travels.

The town from the higher level had no walls but a large force field with oxygen supplies as the architect planned to make the station look nice without any dull massive walls closing the aera.

They needed to have people feel welcome to Osram Stars, not in a typical way of a generic space station. Osram Stars was a refreshing place for all to enjoy, and a place that showed how massive our galaxy really was.

The level on the top of the town had lanterns, flags from different cultures, and wide gates. There was even an area with trees and beaches: the Park.

While you could say Osram Stars was a fair enough distant location, it was a pretty wild environment. There were shady deals going on in some of the most quiet of places, so Osram Stars wasn't always the brightest of things you could imagine.

Not too far off, a damaged ship came to one of the docking pads outside the town. It hovered very steadily as it came in for the landing. It was a classified Olean-Flay: a shiny green vessel. It had yellow lights and had washy noises as it landed.

This was the Mercent Siblings' ship. Well, their recent one. They took it for a spin while making a chase from the rebellious Exdrem for stealing and trespassing.

They barely got out of there alive, which caused their ship to take heavy fire. They knew if they kept doing this, and if they were in more intense chases, they might lose their lives.

They came out of their ship and entered Osram Stars for the first time.

First, there was Alex: the somewhat rebel leader who said that he was in charge but none of his siblings agreed on that. He had daggy blue clothes that didn't really match and wore a headband. Mostly he was a hippie.

Next was Lilly, who would have taken that leader role but was second in command. She had straight, painted, short red hair that stood out from the rest. She wore a light green sleeveless jacket and sleek black boots.

And finally, there was Benny, a wild hair blondie who got it from his sister's side before she dyed it. Besides Alex and Lilly - who were more rebellious and easily argued with each other - Benny was not so helpful with stuff, but he tried to drag them away from any trouble.

The problem with the Mercent Siblings was you didn't know what sort of trouble you would get into. The reason why they called themselves that was that they were runaways who caused mayhem along the way. If you were allies or friends of them, you wouldn't get further in life than being sent for thirty years in a galactic jail, wondering why you ever helped them in the first place. They didn't really have a great list of friends on their radar but have made many enemies instead.

They watched as the town lightened up, while they worried about their ship and how they could repair it. They hadn't come as far as to reach Osram Stars before; it was a very new experience which led one of them to discover.

"This place is incredible!" Benny commented, as he admired the station and its beauty.

"Oh no," Lilly moaned, as both she and Alex were thinking more about their ship as it looked in real bad shape. "I don't know how we could take off with this thing without blowing it up."

"Don't worry about it," Alex told her, quite relaxed, "we'll get a pack of repairs, stay here for a little while and get out."

Benny looked back and forward between the siblings and the town as he couldn't tell what to be focussed on the most.

"Can we just admire the place for once before you two start arguing again?" Benny asked hopefully. "Hey, what happened to our big alien butler?"

"Oh, he got captured." Lilly mentioned, feeling guilty leaving out that information.

"HE WHAT?!?!"

"I didn't want to bring that up; I know how much it would upset you."

"And you didn't come to it because…?" Alex asked.

Lilly strolled past Alex as she knew he was about to get under her skin. Alex looked at Benny with not quite a pleased face. He walked over to his brother's side, and they started to walk into town.

"Don't you worry Benny. I think one day you can be as reliable as me."

"I thought I was the reliable one?" Benny guessed.

Alex gave an unsure look as he added, "Well, maybe one day."

Benny looked back to the ship one last time, wondering if they could get it fully fixed. But again, maybe there was more for Benny to learn about taking on major roles such as repairs.

Floyd had only one ideal place to go to if he needed time to rethink himself or decide what path he should go on next - and that was Osram Stars. There was a place on the station he knew far too often which was a designer restaurant with bunch of aliens serving food.

What Floyd had heard was that they served the best meals in the galaxy or anywhere if you had a rough day. To Floyd, this was one of those days as he sighed and moped outside.

There was a friend of Floyd's who he saw time and time again every time he went to Osram Stars. His face was all tentacles from above his mouth and beard. His hands were also tentacles. He opened the window out on the street to see if anyone was needing take away, and then he saw Floyd. This strange noodle guy was usually bright and shiny but became unimpressed, mostly whenever Floyd was around.

Floyd was leaning on a stool against the waiting area as his friend John was serving his goods. A squid with spiky doughnuts. It wasn't the best of meals Floyd could have thought of, but it was the best option he could think of for today.

"What can I do without getting into anything so action packed?" Floyd asked his alien friend who listened, just listened. "As I repeatedly said, I can't go back to the Library. I know LO-NO would kill me on sight if I take one step inside."

He knew robots like LO-NO didn't have a code to assassinate anyone. But he still had nowhere else to go. Besides arriving at the one place where you could find your way around if you ever got lost.

The alien didn't mind listening; that's all he could do as he didn't talk. He just kept listening until he could get on with his day.

"I mean, John. Can I have a tag that says, 'I'm not up for any major nonsense today, please come another time?' I just wanted to go somewhere where I could lay low, chill, and have no worries in the universe, you know?"

John couldn't give sudden feedback; the only feedback he could give was an unimpressed look at Floyd, as if he deeply understood what Floyd's issues were. They're friendship came as strange at first, but Floyd knew John could be his most significant support if anything went not his way.

"No bringing me into whatever trouble is ahead of me or getting caught into one of them. I need a day off!" Floyd spoke dreamily rather than moping, which drove him into a thought which struck his senses. "No wait! A week! Yes, a week! If I could just take a break for a week, I won't have to complain again!"

John walked away as he had better customers to serve than this one. He shook his head as he really thought he was befriending the biggest fool in the universe.

The siblings were in town where everything was brightened up and fully decorated. The floor was a red brick road, with trees on the sides and streetlamps guiding light so no area could be cast out by the dark. They could also spot stores opening and offering some unique products.

"This is amazing!" Benny commented as he witnessed a new world unfolding in front of him.

"Where are we?" Lilly asked as she spotted very shady locals all over the place earlier, and not taking full trust of the place by the friendly vibe it was offering.

Alex walked over to a sign for this district, which had the usual vibe like the rest of the station. "Reed Town District?" Alex read clearly. "Was this called Ton Town?"

"I thought it was Five Plus Nine with Trolls?" Lilly added with faded memories.

"Nah, I think it was before trolls and before they could count."

"With music instruments??" Benny asked.

"They were doing music before all this." Alex corrected his brother as he stared at the sign and flicked his hand. "Something isn't right."

"What?" Lilly asked behind Alex. "You think this place was invaded?"

Alex scratched his sharp chin as his head leaned back to figure out why this sign was so familiar. They had gone to so many different space stations that they forgot they had been to and may have been somewhere which was identical.

It took Alex quite a while until Benny and Lilly noticed something.

Benny came closer to his brother's ear, "Alex."

"Not now."

"Haven't you noticed it now?"

"Noticed what?"

"Our wallets have been stolen."

"What?!" Alex looked at Benny in shock as he turned around to check his pocket. But Benny was right, they had been robbed! "Where are they?!"

"See those guys over there," Benny pointed, "the ones in blue?"

"Why are they standing there?" Alex asked as he stared curiously at them.

"Oh, because they are terrible robbers."

The siblings chased after the thugs, as the robbers noticed them and then sprinted through the crowd. The thugs were totally out of their league and the siblings had no chance to gain on them. The siblings didn't compete in the Olympic games, but they did know how to run. Every time the blue thugs turned around, they kept seeing that the siblings were on their tail. They were entirely blue, but they didn't have a face; instead, they had goggles - except one of them who wore a simple yellow T-shirt that he got from a gift shop from his home world. They also had funny squirting sounds when they walked.

Floyd was still outside the restaurant, waiting to pick up his takeaway meal. John popped his head out again and noticed Floyd was still there.

"I think I got it!" Floyd said rethinking his plan, as though he liked it very much. "I might stay here! Nothing bad happens here in Osram Stars."

"Not now," John thought.

"Besides, there's a lot to do here." Floyd continued. "There are levels I haven't visited yet, a basketball club I can join, a bunch of other activities I can sign up for, the pool. I say, this isn't half bad."

John shut his window and left Floyd as the only remaining customer outside.

Floyd noticed the window closed and called, "Hello?" he said, a bit confused. "Hellllo?"

Not so far away, the thugs kept up their sprint as people avoided them running past. They took different turns which weren't very effective. The Mercent Siblings were still on their trace, and they wouldn't leave without what was theirs. Then they turn into a street where Floyd was.

Floyd was distracted about his meal and wasn't aware of what was coming towards him.

"John?!" he called out. "I need my meal!!!"

Floyd walked back from his stool. When he looked on his left, the thugs and Floyd clashed as they fell on the ground. The Mercent Siblings came over and stopped as they saw their robbers had been caught.

The thugs were on Floyd as the Librarian had little clue what was happening. He looked at the robbers and noticed the yellow T-Shirt one thug was wearing was cut, and through it were wires and metal.

"Oh no," Floyd moped. "Why did it have to be robots…?"

The robots suddenly shut themselves down and everyone knew they wouldn't power back up anytime soon. The siblings came over and looked at the chaos as Floyd seemed to be stuck.

"Uh, help?"

3.   A Beginning of a Beautiful Friendship

It was for several hours that Benison was sleeping on his cruise ship, the La-Gold. He was the ship's captain with a bunch of crewmen and passengers who wanted to see the stars across the galaxy.

He had recently heard good reviews about his tour and why people were joining the La-Gold. The people here were very happy; the ones that weren't got booted off.

The captain's butler arrived in his chamber as he tried to get his captain off his rich cosy bed and tell him some urgent news. The chamber had a giant window where the captain could see the dark purple side of the galaxy, which had no purpose on this tour because the universe just didn't care.

"What is it, Union?" the captain asked as he rubbed his eyes, getting rid of any sleep. He had no basic hair but shady eyebrows and a brown beard to compensate for that.

"Sir, we have some news from the cargo room," the butler explained. By his appearance, he didn't look much different than a regular butler; he had a pointy moustache and short hair.

"I hope the Hip-Hopping kids aren't on board again!" the captain moaned, imagining the trouble couldn't get any worse. "This is a tour ship, not some show-off show."

"Yes sir, quite right sir." Union replied, "We uh, heard some reports in the cargo room, which were quite alarming, and, well…".

"And?"

"Well, to keep it short, we got a stow-away."

Benison knew what to do when it came to stow-aways. He asked, "Is there anything else we should know about this?"

"Uh, well…", Union said as his face smirked, "When the men found it, it was small. Sized like a baby."

"So, what's wrong?"

"It grew. Rather fast, sir. And it's starting to eat our crew."

"Just like that?" Benison thought he was now understanding the problem. "Have you told the men to shield or block it off?"

"I did, sir, but the stow-away didn't agree."

"Where is it now?"

"Still in the cargo room, sir."

"Then why are you nagging me from my sleep?"

There was a sudden silence from the butler as he didn't show any facial expression. "I only saw the whole thing on an observation camera."

"Then I think you should do something about the whole thing?" the captain asked the butler.

"Yes, right away, sir!" the Butler buttered off as he left the captain in his own quarters.

After the unexpected scenarios that had recently happened, Floyd finally confronted the Mercent Siblings face to face. But what Floyd really wanted was to stay out of anything that would have pulled him right back into any action.

They came to a quieter side of the station, where they sat on stools as they tried to get a better introduction.

"What brings you here?" Benny asked Floyd.

"Well, uh, you see," Floyd started, as he tried to find the right words, "I was just passing by across the galaxy to find somewhere where I could enjoy myself, and instead what I got was more trouble!"

The siblings sat quite awkwardly for a moment, knowing the feeling and how it usually happened to them every day.

"Us too," Lilly told him honestly, "we always get caught with it wherever we go."

"You too?" Floyd asked them. He had a funny thought that they were all meant to collide with each other.

"Trouble is not really something we try to do, but it always appears to follow us."

"Sometimes, we…", Benny explained but was cut off by serious glares coming from Lilly and Alex, "…oh, nothing. But we really wanted to explore."

"Really?" Floyd thought.

"But it isn't enough."

"And there are bad folks out here in the galaxy," Alex explained. "They have their own problems where we always get involved."

"Wow," Floyd thought surprised, "you have the exact same experience that I always have!"

"Do you ever go somewhere and meet people who drag you into a situation which you know you can't manage?" Lilly tested Floyd.

"And not only the place you're in, but everyone tries to kill you for no reason."

"My point exactly!" Lilly agreed. "Alex, I think we have found our newest member."

"There's isn't a new member," Alex dismissed her harshly. "We're just a band of nobodies going across the galaxy with no idea what mayhem we'll get into."

"But he seems so nice and cool," Benny protested as he seemed to get on with Floyd very well.

They had so much in common: bands, games, secret code names, etc.

"And I say no." Alex went over to his sibling's ears in a quiet volume: "He wouldn't know about the things we do."

"He'll get used to it." Lilly replied as she thought Floyd would figure it out sooner rather than later.

"But what about us?!" Alex protested. "Our entire future, behind a prison cell, unable to contact each other or seek help from the outside."

"But…there's no help," Benny commented.

"Exactly!" Alex said, thinking it very logically. "If we let him on board, he'll likely betray us and think we're just using him to be on one of our escapes."

"Alex," Lilly thought clearly, "can you for once stop thinking of your ego and maybe, I don't know, make a friend for once?"

"Why?"

"Because there's no one else," Benny thought deeply into the void.

Alex stared at him as he knew how Benny got when he was all mopey.

"Alright," Alex said out loud, "you can keep him, but I can't promise we may not have to leave him on a planet."

"Now you're thinking like a real leader," Lilly thought dimly.

"Thank you."

The siblings went back to giving their attention to Floyd, who seemed to be off in his own world. He switched back to reality where his new friends were watching him.

"Oh, hi." Floyd said.

"Floyd, can you think of somewhere where we could go so there's no sign of any trouble we would ever face again?" Alex asked him, which sounded like he was asking the impossible.

Floyd had an idea, but he knew it would mean giving up on his retreat. He needed a week off, a whole week for himself to recover fully. "What sort of place are you looking for?"

"Out of the sector," Benny said.

"No, way out of the sector," Alex corrected him.

"Somewhere where we can get out of all of them," Lilly added.

"Like the galaxy?" Floyd asked them.

"Yeah, but it's impossible," Alex bluffed. "There's no way we can find a way out of the galaxy."

"What about a gateway into more galaxies?" Floyd replied, which drew the siblings' attention with interest.

"Go on," Alex offered.

Floyd raised an eyebrow as he seemed to be getting somewhere quite cleverly and experimental.

"What if I told you that the place actually exists, in our own galaxy, where we can go through them, where they go on forever and forever."

The siblings visualised it dreamily; they looked at each other in a language only they understood. Floyd had no idea what they were saying, which made him nervous.

Then they looked at Floyd. "Floyd, how would you like to join us?" Lilly offered.

Floyd gave a scared look as he tried to protest, "Oh no, I would like to, I do, but…"

"This isn't a chance you can decline," Lilly reminded him. "If you don't see us again, you will be unlikely to find us again."

Floyd had a difficult choice: spending his time relaxing on Osram Stars and not worrying about anything for a week or continue bonding with two and maybe three, people he liked and helping them on a mighty quest.

The thought flicked through the Librarian's head that he was making a very hard choice, which could change the course of his plans.

"ALRIGHT!" he said as he made his decision. "I'll come!"

He shook hands with Lilly and smiled.

"Welcome to the team!" Lilly commented.

"Yay!" Benny celebrated, "We have another member!"

"Ugh," Alex said in disgust as he rolled his eyes; he could hardly think how long this would last.

It was true in fact what the butler had told Captain Benison: the creature was growing quite fast in fact.

It first was once a ball with two legs, then in thirty minutes it turned into a baby sized lizard with bright green dots. In the next hour and a half, it reached its full form: a three feet Rutan with wide feet and four black nails and bendy knees. Its giant hand had three claws but in an odd look. Its face was strange in its appearance, but its teeth gashed all over the face, so you knew right away this beast was going to eat you and beamed at you with yellow eyes.

It wandered through the ship without anyone noticing it, passing through corridors, then back to the cargo room, and then into the shipping dock where it terrorised the crew in the bay.

They wore an all-blue uniform as the crew were unloading the passenger's luggage from their ships; until they saw the Rutan approaching in a slow-paced speed at which they panicked and ran for their lives.

The Rutan roared at them as it tried to raise its big hand at them, but the crew were in the far distance and were moving faster than him. But the very good news about the whole situation right now was that no one had been eaten yet.

Behind the Rutan, without noticing, was a large enough crate that opened its lid. The lid popped out and out of it came two detached robots with one of their bodies.

"WITH ALL THE PLACES HE COULD BE AT, THIS HAS TO BE AT THE TOP OF THE LIST!" guessed the robot LO-NO with a smart of brilliance.

LO-NO's personal assistant, YO-NO, attached himself back together as he picked up the orb head of LO-NO from the ground and held onto it.

"NOW, WE NEED TO SEARCH EVERY ROOM AND CHAMBER ON BOARD IF WE HAVE ANY CHANCE OF FINDING FLOYD. MOST IMPORTANTLY, WE'LL SURPRISE HIM AND TAKE HIM BACK TO THE LIBRARAY!"

"CORRECTION," informed YO-NO, "GOING INSIDE A BOX WOULD BE ALARMED TRASPASS."

"YEAH, AND?"

"IT WOULD'VE DAMAGED ME."

"I'M THE ONE WITH MORE DAMGE!!!" LO-NO shouted. "I'M THE ONE WITHOUT A BODY" LO-NO sighed and then added, "LET'S JUST SNEAK

AROUND THE PLACE WITHOUT BEING CAUGHT."

"AFFIRMTIVE" YO-NO agreed as they took off.

The Mercent Sibling's ship, the Addition Fire, flew light years across deep space, passing planets and more planets, knowing that passing every world or sector would give them a glimpse from this galaxy into the whereabouts of more galaxies.

Floyd had said perfectly that avoiding any world would give them the chance to find the impossible. Avoid what is possible and go forward towards the impossible.

Lilly and Alex were in the piloting room, since they had very good experience when it came to flying ships, but they knew that the ship itself wasn't actually fixed as planned.

Meanwhile Floyd and Benny were in the spare room down below playing a game that they knew too well. It was called Sa-Booth: a board game where you weld cards of your chosen warriors, up to six, in each party as you try to defeat your opponent. There were a D12 dice, emulating cards, a rule book and a card of doom by the Dragon of Death! (A mythical creature that was discovered in 2034.)

"When are you guys coming?" Floyd called to Lilly and Alex to try to get their attention.

"It goes up to eight to nine players," Benny told them.

"See? We need more players," Floyd called out. "I thought Benny was going to play."

"I'm Benny."

"Oh," Floyd spoke, realising his mistake, "then who's the one with the banner on his head who looks like some guy from the 1970s?"

"That's Alex."

"Hippy," Floyd thought, "he is not a traitor, is he?"

"No, Alex's pretty cool," Benny replied as he looked at his cards, "but he does forget to watch out for his manners."

"Ah, the self-doubting type."

"Sorry?"

Floyd looked at Benny as he tried to describe it better. "I can see he is trying to be a good leader, but he forgets he isn't."

"How do you know?" Benny asked, guessing that Floyd must be a mind reader.

"It's just something I could see sometimes," Floyd told Benny as they looked at their cards.

Then, an alarm alerted them, which gave them a surprise. Floyd and Benny weren't sure what to do; they thought it was just a false alarm, so they kept playing.

Then the ship shook as crates and boxes and other stuff slid to one side. They hit the wall as the set pieces of the game fell.

"My Master of Mountains Card!" Benny roared angrily. "I was going to use it to end your reckoning!"

"Oi! Don't spoil the card!" Floyd told him.

Then steam came out of the ship's pipes as everything was ripping apart.

Floyd got up as he tried to hold the nearest pipes with both hands, and tried to attach them before they suffocated without oxygen. Floyd looked around as he found some small handy tool nearby and used it to wrench the pipe. He kept wrenching until another pipe detached itself, and the station situation was becoming more than a false alarm.

"Could you get the other one?" Floyd asked Benny, who was sitting quite uncomfortably on the boxes.

"I could try," Benny replied as he got up. But before Benny could do a thing, a voice came through the speakers. Floyd and Benny didn't know there *were* any speakers on this ship!

"Guys!!!" it was Lilly's voice, and by the tone of her voice, the news wasn't great. "We got incoming!"

4. Boarded by the Beetle Bigrade

A docking clamp linked the Addition Fire to a vast ship, which was five hundred feet wide on each side and was tall enough to fit anything quite massive onboard. To Floyd, who had seen bigger ships before, there was something quite ancient about this one.

They stood looking at the clamps as they all wondered who was boarding them. It made their ship rustle - which could tear apart their ship if their invaders wanted to - but the bigger question was: who was invading?

"Who you think wanted to invade our ship?" Benny asked his brother and sister.

"Hopefully not our enemies," Lilly replied, fearing the worst.

Floyd stared at them, quite puzzled. "You guys have enemies?"

"Yeah, we try to not think about it." Alex told him. Floyd rolled his eyes. Floyd never had enemies he could recall in memory. "They just came out of the blue and locked a beam on us, and there we are."

"I haven't seen anything like this," Lilly commented, as it seemed very unusual. "There shouldn't be a tracker beam if it would blow us up."

"Malfunctions?" Floyd guessed, if that was helpful. "Sorry, I also have no idea what this is."

"Whatever it is, it's going to come out of those doors right now," Alex mentioned as the door flew up.

They all caught a brief look inside the ship, which appeared to be dark with no light. They noticed that this was a widened corridor with some sort of technical buttons and lights flashing on the walls.

They shortly caught the look of their invaders, and they could only see their green glowing eyes. But by the appearance they saw, these invaders must be big beetles, as they were the size of a table.

"WhO ArE yOu?" one the Beetle ordered, with one of its legs sticking up, which was also glowing green. To Floyd and his pals, guessing what it was, it looked like a weapon.

"Honestly, we have no clue what is happening here." Floyd told them he and his pals must be more confused about the situation than they were aware of.

The two beetles stared at them while making a clicking noise which they couldn't help.

"ThIS Is oUR EmPIRE," the Beetle explained, "ThE KARANAk EmPIRE DoES NOT APpRovE UNwELCoME VISTioRs TO oUr EmpIrE!"

"The Karanak Empire?" Alex asked them. "Was that meant to be some sort of serial?"

"Nope, never heard of them." Floyd thought, as he had no records of them in his knowledge.

"SILENCE!!" the Beetle ordered as his sidekick rushed towards them and the humans held their hands. "YOU ARE ORDERED BY OUR QUEEN, to FOLLOW US INtO hER DOMAIN."

"Alright, chill!" Alex told the beetle, walking through the Karanak's ship as the door shut behind them.

They could see quite narrowly as the light dimmed a bit which gave them the ability to see. They all theorised that the Karanaks had darker vision to see through than do other life forms.

They walked to other wide corridors which seemed like a labyrinth as the beetles led them in different turns, where the ship seemed quite the same with nothing new.

While the beetles kept crackling about, Benny thought to ask Floyd something. "What can you tell about these guys?"

Floyd had only a faint guess as he hadn't seen lifeforms like this before. "Not something I could summarise, sorry," he acknowledged.

"I say when we have the chance, we slam down these beetles and get the heck out of here!" Alex told them in a quiet volume so that the beetles couldn't hear.

"WE WILL NOT LET OUR PRISONERS BE SET FREE SO EASILY," the beetle in the front row commented, "THAT'S RIGHT. THE KARANAK HAVE EXCELLENT HEARING. YOU REALLY THINK WE WOULD BE FOOLED BY ANY PRIMITIVE?"

"Why does he think we're primitive?" Benny asked, hurt as he thought the bugs were insulting them.

"Its…it's just what they think Benny," Lilly told him. "Just go along with it."

The beetles soon took them to the ship's main basement, where the ship squared out to become no longer wide corridors, but a vast chamber with a bunch of beetles roaming around. There were about two floor levels that the beetles were at as they could climb the walls to reach places.

There were pits with control units for the beetles to use to pilot the ship. But in the centre, which caught the humans by surprise, was their queen.

The queen had the body of any other humanoid but had the features of the beetles. She was about five times larger than them with six arms and bendy legs. The face had the same beetle mouth and eyes as the rest.

She seemed very strange and not very normal to anything they have encountered. She sat on a throne in the centre of a huge nest. The humans glared at her, quite terminated.

"*YOU HAVE TRASPASSED INTO OUR LAND!*"
the queen spoke quite strangely. "*WE DO NOT ALLOW
STRANGERS TO COME AND INVADE OUR
TERRITORY.*"

"Well, if you could've put up a sign to say so,
that would've been useful," Benny told her, to which his
siblings tried to quiet him down.

"*YOU DARE QUESTION OUR WAYS?!*" the
Queen roared, as that comment was an insult to their
kind. "*WE SEEK ONLY ISOLATION FROM THE REST
OF THE COSMOS. WE DO NOT WANT ANY SORT OF
AFFAIRS WITH ANYONE, NOT EVEN YOU!*"

"So you say," Floyd said to the queen, as he tried
to get her attention focussed on him. "Now, tell me.
What brings you all the way out here?"

"*ISOLATION, ITS OUR WAY TO REMAIN IN
HIBERNATION FOR OUR SPIECES.*"

"Like…making more beetles?" Alex thought in
disgust.

Later, a tube sprung up near where Floyd was,
and inside it had bubbling blue water. Inside that was a
smaller beetle which everyone could see was a baby
after he hatched from an egg.

"*ITS ONLY FOR THE NEW BREED TO START
FEEDING INTO THE COSMOS. SO, WE MUST SURVIVE
AND MAINTAIN OUR FUTURE.*"

"So, let me get this right," Floyd told the queen as he tried to connect all the dots, but there were lots of dots in the room. "You're starving here, only to start a new evolution of the Karanak. And you're trying to make more beetles to roam around on this ship. Then what?"

"THEN WE SHALL FIND A NEW WORLD AND A NEW ERA OF THE KARANAK SHALL BEGIN!"

"And that will be lots of fun," Benny replied, quite scared of the queen's tone.

"And what are we then?" Alex asked the important details. "How do we fit in the picture?"

The queen seemed quite focussed on Alex and his siblings after he asked that. The beetles crackled as their attention was drawn to the humans. To Floyd's knowledge, the signs weren't good.

"WE SAID THAT WE NEED TO FEED. YOU ARE OUR RESOURCES."

The beetles headed towards the Mercent Siblings and surrounded them. The siblings were quite out of their league as they tried to keep their distance. Floyd was watching this until he noticed he was in a similar predicament like them. He backed away as the beetles crawled towards him.

"Okay," he said quite nervously, "let's just reconsider about all this?"

Then Floyd noticed near him tubes were over a wall. He also noticed some type of controls that even the librarian could describe had the look of a device.

He leapt forward and pressed some buttons. Suddenly the lighting of the ship flashed red as Floyd must have set off an alarm. The beetles were all screeching as others ran about seeming to increase their numbers.

"That's me done!" Floyd called as he ran towards the siblings who had a clearer vision of the place. The beetles chased after them, crawling over the walls.

Meanwhile, the queen had other problems in hand. "I NEED SOMEONE TO CHECK ON THE LEFTOVERS! I DO HOPE THEY'RE NOT RUNNING STALE."

The humans rushed through the corridors as they had to memorize where they came from. But what gave them more of a problem was that the beetles were gaining on them. They followed their instincts to recall the way, but sometimes they noticed the beetles had found quicker ways to reach them, so they had to move fast.

A horde of the beetles came out as the humans appeared through the corridors. The siblings had to move away from them as the creatures crawled near them.

The humans finally found the exit to their ship, as they raced towards it. A bunch or nearly hundreds of beetles were just behind them. When they reached in the ship, they had to close the doors in maximum speed.

Lilly slammed her hand onto the door button, which shielded out all the beetles who all clashed together. But she couldn't think about them right now.

"We have to fly out of here!" she called out to her brother, Alex.

"Yep!" he replied as he didn't have time for any feedback. They all headed into the pilot room where they tried to take off. Luckily, the tracker beam wasn't on them anymore. The Karanak's technology must be very old and rusty, meaning it was much easier to escape out of their grasp.

The Addition Fire flew out from next to the Karanak Mothership and tried to take off at max speed. But canons from the Karanak's ship fired as there was a bunch of them firing green lasers at the Addition Fire.

"Firing?! Firing?! Oh, that's just great!" Alex thought. "So outrageous!"

"I thought we were out of their league?!" Benny thought that was the end of their encounter.

"Benny, I don't think every trouble we have been in would always be the end." Lilly commented as she dodged the ship to avoid incoming fire. The Karanak

Mothership soon gained a small speed on the Addition Fire. It wasn't fast but it was following their lead.

As each blast zoomed towards the Addition Fire, explosions boomed as the Addition looped and swirled around. They weren't getting far away from the Mothership.

The humans watched as they noticed the Karanak were right with them, not losing any trace.

"We're not losing them!" Lilly said. She needed to find a way to escape quickly.

The Addition Fire spiralled around, as they passed a number of lasers coming in front or behind them. They watched in horror.

But the Karanak ship was moving towards them, and the Addition Fire noticed that they were getting nearer. No matter what tactics they could do, they would still be in the same dead-end loop.

"Wait stop!" Floyd called out. "What if we increase the hyper speed and try to push through its limits?"

The Siblings stared at him quite stunned.

"Nah!" Alex commented. "You know this ship is badly defective."

"If it would have got us killed?!" Lilly told Alex. "We could take a chance like that rather than being blown to pieces!"

"I think Lilly's right," Benny agreed with his sister's methods. "If we stay out here with them, we will be dead!"

"Yeah, I don't want that thought in my head." Alex said.

"Increase the speed to full power and drop everything else!" Floyd advised the gang.

But the gang had a troubling thought.

"But that would leave the ship to drain!" Benny recalled. "We won't have any power left to fly this ship anymore!"

"Then we'll figure that bit out afterwards!"

Lilly did as Floyd advised, as even Alex was afraid of Floyd's idea. They set the ship to go into hyper speed which meant they needed to power down a few of the ship's systems - which would burst out the ship's core.

Then, VOM! They blasted out of the sector and the Addition Fire was leading them across light years, passing planets and stars as they went, leaving them shaken about what would come next…

5.   Kailyn: Planet of the Open Sky

Lights and stars flashed through their window, as the speed was so intense that no one could move a bone, or even a finger. The ship powered down as it managed to find a nearby habitable planet.

They arrived on the world of Kailyn - a blue jungle world with a pink sky - as the day dimmed down after its two suns. One was still hovering as the day was coming to an end.

But by seeing the wonderful environment, the crew had a problem, which Benny noticed clearly.

"Uh ho," he said very slowly.

"What?!" Floyd asked him.

Benny gave a nervous look which made everyone look at him, until they started to hear shattering noises within the ship.

"What was that?" Lilly responded.

Then Benny finally gave out.

"Just letting you know: remember when we parked the ship back on the space station and I was going to tell the repair crew to recharge the ship to at least 86% and give them some changes which FYI: I didn't?"

The sound grew louder as it was coming around from different parts of the ship. It grew more serious as the crew noticed that whatever Benny did, he should have done something first before having this scenario.

"Smell that refreshing sea," Benny sighed, as he tried to put his mind on something else other than noticing the danger they were in.

"Why can't I smell sea?" Floyd noticed.

"Because there's no sea nearby," Lilly told him, as she looked at Benny madly. "Benny, what did you do?"

"I totally didn't recharge it," Benny said guilty.

The ship dropped and was heading towards the forest. Lilly pulled it up while pink leaves dashed as she tried to get the ship to hover up.

"Okay! I didn't mean for that to be so out there!" Benny commented, "I had no money…"

"We only have about less than one percent of power!!!!" Alex snapped. "We're about to die and I am hearing excuses right now?!?!?!"

The ship came above the trees as they noticed another problem. A rocky wall of a cliff was coming dead ahead, and they need to pull up in the next ten seconds.

Benny pressed a button which Alex told him not to, but he did it anyway. The ship flung up and spun to the surface, flying through the trees - which part of the wildlife watched in confusion.

Alex looked at his brother with an astonished look. "You pressed it."

"What was that?" Floyd asked as he didn't know what that button was meant for.

Then a bright light bloomed from the back of the ship as they were diving down once more. They braced for their landing as the ship crashed into some branches of a few trees. Windows started to crack, and the ship took some hit from it, but the ship stopped as it appeared to be stuck.

Alex checked if there was any power left. It was a shame that there wasn't. He replied to his crew, "OK, that's issue one solved."

"What's issue two?" Floyd asked cluelessly.

"We have to jump."

They got out of the ship steadily and carefully. They climbed down onto a tree, which wasn't easy as a challenge, but the Mercent Siblings had done many trials like this in many environments, so they knew the ropes well. Floyd, on the other hand, didn't, so each sibling had to give him advice.

Blue leaves flowed downward as they watched the forest in full view. It was incredible and breathtaking seeing the massive tree landscape wherever you looked. Hills and long surface grass loamed in every direction, but there always appeared to be some cliffs near ahead.

Lilly instructed Floyd on his steps, where he should put his feet on which part of the tree, as she could easily spot that he was struggling. At one moment, he came to a stumble as she quickly instructed "Put your right foot over that line mark over there!"

Floyd did it exactly and quickly caught his breath. "Phew," he let out, "how are you lot knowing how to climb so well? You don't seem to be the climbing lot."

"We're not," Lilly told Floyd. "It's just whatever gets thrown at us in life, we had to come through some challenges."

"And you had to overcome them?" Floyd asked, which reminded him of when he escaped Tasha. "I've done something like that; wasn't easy though. Had to make an escape by blowing myself thousands of feet from an exploding volcano."

"You're joking!" Benny asked from below.

"Yeah, my plan was so extreme that I had to minimise what I could work with."

"Wow!" Benny thought, as his excitement couldn't cool down. "It's like we've got a real action hero with us!"

"I wouldn't go that far," Floyd mentioned as he took another step down.

"I don't think I would do something so intense as that," Lilly responded, as she thought Floyd must have pushed further to get here.

Then, they could hear some rocking from the ship. It tilted as it dropped down by the tight vines around it. It passed them as it crashed down a hundred feet and burst into flames.

Everyone watched in horror.

"Ahhhh!" Benny screamed awkwardly. "We made it out of that one."

Then Alex noticed Benny was carrying a backpack on his back, which gave Alex an unimpressed thought on what it was.

"Benny, did you really just bring Sa-Booth with you?"

"Yes!" Benny called, "with supplies too, duh!"

Alex shook his head, as they continued climbing down the big, massive tree.

6.   A Day on Kailyn

The sky was growing dark as the second blue sun of Kailyn was going down. The gang made camp further in the forest, near the hills, where they could see, a few feet away, loaming rocky towers near a cliff.

At the camp, it was more natural, with the trees being so tall they reached nearly a hundred feet. They could also hear echoes within them. Some type of special effect they had? Probably.

"What is that I've been hearing in the last hour?" Lilly asked. She had been taking notice, while Alex was busy meditating and Benny was off finding dinner – or to see if he could get dinner anyway.

While there wasn't anyone to attend to this conversation, Floyd coughed as he spoke. "I thought it was some kind of birds talking to one another, but I'm guessing that maybe that there's something up there whispering to one another."

Lilly gave Floyd a curious look as she added, "Go on."

Floyd did. "I'm not sure what they're saying, really. Are they unhappy that they have some unwelcome visitors onto their planet? Don't they like us as our ship went boom and nearly tried to kill them?"

"I am pretty sure that wasn't our intention."

"But they might have their own ideas and opinions on us since we arrived."

"Floyd, please stop talking." Lilly told him, which he did.

Then Benny made it back to the others as he couldn't find any food that would not have escaped or tried to kill him. He slammed down on the bluegrass floor as in front of it lay the game Sa-Booth. He rubbed his hands in excitement.

"OK, now, where were we?"

"Maybe not tonight, Benny," Floyd apologised.

Benny gave a sad and disappointed expression. He looked at Alex, who was too focussed on his pointless exercises, then at Lilly.

"Don't look at me!" she replied.

"Then, in that case, I'll play by myself," he said as he drew cards from the pile.

In the kitchen of the La-Gold, the Ratan terrorized his way to the chefs that were busy cooking as they didn't sign up to be eaten.

Three chefs had already been eaten by the creature as it angers for food.

"EATTTT!!!!" it called out.

"You won't get anything from me!" said one of the chefs as he threw a carrot at the beast but missed.

The chefs backed away from the beast as they had to barricade themselves and keep a good distance. A tension of horror filled in for the innocent cooks as they didn't want to be eaten.

"Oh boy," said the scared top chef as he watched the monster approaching nearer. "And here we thought we already had so many passengers on board that we need to feed. Where is the security!"

On the floor, near the Rutan, one of the android chefs got his arm torn off by the creature. He wasn't impressed with what happened.

"It wasn't cheap you know!" he yelled at the creature.

The Ratan continued to roar at the cooks until the backup crew with Union the Butler came to assist. The backup crew wore sleek grey suits with goggles. They were holding a long freezing rods that were attached with round packs on their backs.

"Now, this is the stow-away that was wandering through the ship," the butler commented while carrying an old-fashioned pistol. He studied the creature's facial expression so he may guess what it wanted, but then it roared in the butler's face.

The backup crew were startled from the roar as they shivered and took a step back. They got ready to strike whenever the creature moved, but it just stood.

The butler looked at the creature up and down as he replied, "I would have taken you back to the cargo, but since you're here…", Union was trying to figure out what to do with it, then an idea struck him. "I say, what if I take you to your room instead? And maybe we could work out our differences?"

"EAAATTTTTT!!!!!!"

"Ah, delightful!"

"But it ate my cooks!" said the chef outraged.

"And my arm!" said the android as he lifted up his torn off arm.

"Oh, that's your worry, then," the butler told them unfairly.

"But how are we meant to cook more if we're three and a half short?" the chef asked.

"Again, not our problem."

Underneath the kitchen table, inside one of the carpets, were LO-NO and YO-NO, who were there the whole time as they tried not to be noticed. They were all over themselves as their bodies hit and clanged into each other.

"I WISH YOU COULD GET OFF ME BEFORE ANYONE NOTICES US!" LO-NO told his half-brother. "WE'RE IN SERIOUS TROUBLE HERE!"

"WE ARE IN A PLACE OF SAFETY," YO-NO disagreed. "THIS IS THE PERFECT PLACE AWAY FROM ANY NEAR DANGER"

"HAVEN'T YOU NOTICED THAT THE BACKUP CREW IS RIGHT HERE IN FRONT OF US!" LO-NO looked out at their shoes. "IF THEY SAW US, THEY WOULD USE US FOR TARGET PRATICE!"

"PRECISELY!"

"NOT PRECISELY! THAT'S NOT WHAT I SAID!" then, through the cupboard door, LO-NO caught something out at the corner which appeared to be a robotic droid like them who was part of the pickup crew team. It caught LO-NO by excitement as he saw the shiny black and gold form it inhabited which seemed so magnificent with its beauty.

"HEY! HEY!", LO-NO whispered to YO-NO to get his attention, "YO-NO! DO YOU SEE THAT?"

"IT IS A VABRICK ANDRIOD DATACLASS..."

"I KNOW THAT. CAN YOU GET US OUT OF HERE SO WE COULD AMBUSH IT?"

"SURE, LO-NO, WHAT DO YOU HAVE IN MIND?"

"I'M GOING TO GET INTO HIS HEAD!"

Floyd was dreaming that he was in a mythical forest, just like the one he was in. The night sky filled with light and glittering stars with shades of pinkish purple dust flowing about into the cosmos.

As Floyd stood about, the treetops glowed in a luminating light blue as well as a purple line trail on the grass.

But Floyd felt weird, as he knew this shouldn't be real but for some reason it was in a way. His eyes glowed deep bright blue and his body was becoming invisible as purple patterns lined all around him.

Then, he saw a deer with big antlers and sharp crystal spikes coming from its legs. The body was blue with green lines from the top part of the body as well as from its legs. Its eyes were as light blue as Floyd's, but they glowed even brighter.

Floyd had no idea what it was, a magical beast that somehow was making a mental link with him? He had heard few stories of some creatures like this in the archive. The Tinbeas?

Floyd didn't know what to do as the deer just stood there, waiting for the librarian's presence to follow. Floyd took few feet while the deer turned to the opposite direction for him to follow. He rushed towards the deer while floating flowers hovered as Floyd dove deeper.

They journeyed through the forest as the deer stopped and Floyd watched. In the sky were planets that were swirling all around and moving very jumbly; they seemed to come so close without making the hemisphere shake.

But as Floyd saw a few feet away from the deer was bunch of zigged lines where all the planets were drawn towards and also spat out of. He could also see a portal inside it as he gazed upon galaxies and more galaxies.

Oh gosh, what had he come to? What making of creation is this? This meant so much to the frightened and terrified Librarian as he sensed the energy it was drawing was absorbing Floyd in. The gravity pulled at him and parts of the grass to fly in; pieces of the earth rippled and distorted, but it had no effect on the deer. Floyd gripped his hold onto the grass as he looked at the deer who stared right in him, and he begged the deer to help him, but no.

Floyd woke up in a startle as the same deer from his dream appeared in front of him, except the eyes weren't glowing blue and nor was any of the other features of its body glowing.

Floyd gasped as he dropped down on the ground. It was daylight in the sunny morning and Floyd had to wonder how this creature arrived from his dream.

"Good morning!" Lilly told the frightful Floyd as she was packing the leftovers they had from last night.

Floyd was full of questions and nerves.

"Uhh…" Floyd tried to speak before the deer frowned at him, and the librarian felt that if he moved a muscle, the deer would lick him to death. "Where did the deer come from?" he said, scared.

"Oh, he was there all morning," Benny replied. "A bunch of his friends came with him; they came here to chill."

"A bunch?" Floyd asked, worried. "What are they doing here?"

The deer moved away from Floyd as the librarian crawled his way to where Alex was meditating over a pile of rocks.

The pack of the Radiant Deer were eating rows of apples over a tree branch. The chewing distracted Alex as he tried to block out their appearance.

"I don't mind wildlife coming here to relax, but I do have a problem when they keep me unfocussed," he said harshly.

Lilly came up to one of the deer to pat and an idea sparked through her head.

"Hey, I have an idea!" she told the gang. "Why don't we explore the place and maybe play a bit of our version of hockey?"

"With deer?" Floyd asked.

"Yes," she said, as she was looking for a challenge.

Floyd had to think if he would like to accept that task; he came out with, "I'm not an expert on hockey or riding off-world animals."

"I can teach you," she told him. Floyd's confidence seemed to settle, at least with someone who had his back.

"Okay then," he said.

They hopped on a separate deer each. As they rode them, they looked back to the brothers.

"Aren't you coming?"

"Sorry," Benny said, disappointed. "I have to find something that can get us off this planet."

"You two have fun," Alex replied with his eyes still closed.

Lilly shook her head as she and Floyd rode out.

"It's his relaxation therapy. It's one of the most important things that my brother loves to enjoy."

"Ah," Floyd nodded, "I noticed that he is quite dull when he speaks. He appears to say something without having any care involved."

"How do you know?" Lilly asked Floyd, thinking he had such incredible insight.

"It's just something I could see sometimes," he said, as they rode further into the forest.

Floyd and Lilly strolled through the forest and passed through the tall trees, that appeared to echo around them. The sounds weren't very loud but kept repeating while they passed by.

Even though it did fascinate Floyd, he was pretty nervous about how these Radiant Deer would react to off-worlders; he kept thinking about that dream. While he looked down, he noticed straight ahead that long branches from the trees wacked him in the face.

Lilly had experience with off-world wildlife: she knew which animal would not threaten or kill them. This was one of her specialties she learnt about over the years. She got the deer to speed up as Floyd caught them; she wanted to know much about these creatures before they started playing.

Alex was alone. All the silence and peace with no one talking about, or any distractions. The campsite was quiet and empty as everyone left, including the pack of Radiant Deer. He was finally in peace.

Exactly what he wanted, isolation. The thought claimed him deeply, as there wasn't any other better activity that he should anticipate or have any care for.

Then he heard blooming birds flying above the trees and air blowing in his direction. It was something he was happy to hear, nothing to be bothered by.

But he noticed at that moment, that over in the trees, tiny whispers were talking to each other. It seemed they were making fun of him, and Alex didn't like being making fun of.

Lilly and Floyd both took out long sticks as they stood seventy feet apart from each other on their deer. There were stone lines behind them which represented a goal, and in the centre lay a pebble.

Lilly took the upper hand as she had a clear advantage against the librarian. She pin-pointed where the pebble was as she swung her stick and hit it over into Floyd's goal.

Floyd tried his best to control his deer while trying to make a shot but missed and caused the deer to stop harshly. Floyd apologised as he tried to focus on the game. Floyd tried to make some wins but only made a fool of himself as he kept making the same mistake.

Meanwhile, Lilly kept winning points as Floyd kept trying to win a single point. By what the librarian could see, she had some skill. While Lilly kept scoring, Floyd sighed in disbelief.

"Come on. We're losing here," he told the deer who bluffed in selfishness.

Floyd thought he would do his best in the next couple of rounds as he dashed his deer towards the pebble while Lilly made her way to it. She got her stick on the pebble before Floyd could touch it. Lilly passed across the field before making another goal.

Floyd once again headed to the pebble, but Lilly always seemed to get to it first. At one point Floyd accidently fell off the deer and crashed onto the grass.

Lilly scored few more goals, then she called a win. She raised her stick with both hands in the air.

"Woohoo!" she called out, celebrating. "I win!"

"Well, you beat me fair and square," Floyd commented as he tried not to let out his full feelings. "I have to say, I think you may have better experience than me."

"Well, I have better experience than my brothers too," Lilly revealed, which Floyd undoubtably understood, "but I think you have some good skills too."

"Yeah, well, knowledge does have its uses," Floyd mentioned.

Then, they heard a rustle coming their way. What they saw was Benny who was riding his deer with Alex on the back.

"Ah, there you guys are," Benny replied happily.

"Benny, what's wrong?" Lilly asked him.

"Well, I think I had better show you."

7.   On Board the Finest Cruise Ship in the Galaxy

Benny brought everyone over to an area of tall mountains with strange pattern shapes which beamed the sunlight towards them. Benny took out a shiny and thin gold black card with a peculiar logo on the back.

"I found this at this spot," Benny commented. The place seemed more than deserted. "I have no idea who would have left this behind."

"The better question isn't who left it behind Benny, but why is it here?" Lilly replied as she grabbed the card and studied it.

Floyd had speculations drifting through his head about how it appeared here. "Maybe someone came to check the place out?"

"But it's a level zero planet; maybe a level one," Alex replied. "But the point is there's nothing for anyone to check around."

"Or maybe if they were passengers or crew members from a cruise ship called the La-Gold," Lilly said, as she read more details in the other part of the card which was all blue with text written all over it.

They all studied it until a small hologram head appeared from the card.

Hello! Welcome to the La-Gold! The finest cruise all across the galaxy! We have been recommended as one of the top bests cruise ships as people seem to not to get enough of our wonderful experiences.

We want to take you across the incredible sectors, throughout the cosmos, and to see many beautiful sceneries, where only the La-Gold can take you.

We also have many ranges of activities and entertainment that our passengers can enjoy. We have a long hall art gallery, a cinema room, an open theatre and our dinning area where everyone can enjoy our bests meals on offer.

We also have options for anyone who wanted to visit any uninhabitable planet. If you are stranded in any unexpected scenario, please press this gold button as it will take you straight back to our cruise.

And we hope you'll enjoy the experience!

The face winked as it disappeared. They all looked at the gold button at the bottom of the card. Then they had some thoughts.

"Do you think we could go on board while we're not passengers?" Floyd asked.

"Sure, we're passengers!" Alex replied as if Floyd was speaking nonsense. "One ticket to get out of this place."

"Alex is right," Lilly agreed. "I don't even know how this got here, but I'm happy it did. This could be our only exit."

Benny gave an unsure look as he added, "Well, I was kinda liking being here. But I haven't been on a cruise for a while."

"And I do want to be on the finest cruise in the galaxy," Floyd commented.

"Never heard of the La-Gold," Alex said with lack of knowledge.

Lilly, still holding the card glared at it as she said, "Then I can see only one thing to do."

Lilly pressed the button, and hovering gold rings appeared and surrounded them as they were beamed up.

Then the next thing they knew, they were on a wide length pad with a small staircase. As they walked down, they saw other pads the same that lined up. They appeared in a long hall with red carpet and paintings on the walls.

A crowd of people wandered through the hall as they were either studying the paintings or were trying to reach to another part of the ship.

The ship looked very rich, and the people must have paid a fortune just to be here. Well, they did say it was the finest cruise ship in the galaxy, which meant more than paying for an average budget.

"Wowowowowowowowow!" Benny commented. He couldn't contain himself with the details of the ship. Everything seemed so wonderous and so refreshing. He guessed that if he popped his head into another room, he might get the exact same response.

"So, this is the La-Gold?" Alex commented as he noticed the passengers walking by. "Are they wearing rich people's clothes?"

"Looks like it," Floyd said as the Mercent Siblings stared back at him and studied his robe. Floyd looked maybe nearly the same as them besides the different clothing he was wearing.

"It looks like you may be more fashion-less than the rest of us," Alex said, disapproving.

"This is made by some of the most fabulous of materials and style," Floyd acknowledged without getting insulted.

Then they noticed a holographic image of the different planets, stars and sectors of the galaxy showing where the cruise was going. They walked up to it to get a better view.

Welcome! said the same voice from before. *These fine stars of the Derkin System have been abandoned with shades of light, knowing in fifty years, that they'll brighten for…*

The talk was getting very boring for Alex and Lilly as they walked apart in different directions, while Floyd and Benny were left alone together.

Then Benny noticed a couple of minutes later that they were gone.

"Uh…guys?"

In a stuffy room with lockers and hanged crew uniforms, YO-NO and LO-NO tied the Android in a chair as a cable was plugged between both its and LO-NO's heads.

LO-NO was downloading himself into the android, while sending the android's data to some storage system so that anyone could find him and plug him into a new body.

LO-NO was very excited to take control; the detail was smooth and breath-taking. The toes and fingers were gold with the black hands attached. The body shined and the head was nearly identical to his but more 'out there'.

A row of numbers dialled randomly on LO-NO's and the android's screens as LO-NO could feel the progress commencing. Then, as the full download was complete, LO-NO was inside the body, and he spotted his old head laying on the ground. It was cold and lifeless, and he felt almost empty for leaving it.

But LO-NO could finally feel since it seemed like an eternity; something to move, without shouting at someone and giving demands to do simple tasks that LO-NO could do.

He felt more and felt like something had returned.

"NOW THIS IS MORE LIKE IT!" LO-NO said in glory, "YO-NO, UNTIE ME!"

YO-NO did so as LO-NO raised both arms carefully and started to wiggle his fingers. It seemed everything was working as normal, but he seemed to forget how to move or how it worked. It had been twenty years since he had a body and he thought he should relearn his steps.

Before he took his first step, he fell out of his chair and clashed into the floor with his head.

"YOU HAVE BEEN DESTORYED", YO-NO acknowledged.

"NO, YOU FOOL," LO-NO replied as he slowly got back up and stood wonkily. Then he managed to walk one step at a time. "IT WAS JUST A BIT OF A STUMBLE. THANK GOODNESS I'M OUT OF THAT THING," looking at his old robot body.

While there were a lot of things that YO-NO wasn't ready to be programmed for - he was more designed to socialise, even to ask important subjects - he asked, "BUT THAT WAS YOUR HEAD, WAS IT NOT?"

LO-NO stared back to the orb, and he did feel a loss without it.

"WELL, NOT ANYMORE," he replied. "NOW, LET'S START EXPLORING, SHALL WE?"

The La-Gold was much more than a cruise commercial; it was a massive scale ship with massive halls, incredible dining rooms, a pool room, and a dome-like scenery room. No matter where you went onboard, there was always something that sparked with richness.

Floyd and Benny visited as many of the rooms as possible; they even saw part of a talent show at the theatre from a balcony. They arrived at a large hall where they studied a giant sculpture of an alien that seemed nearly like a scorpion with a dolphin fin head. In one hand was an apple while in the other was a handbag with feathers sticking out. No one knew what this was meant to represent; even what the feathers were that this creature was taking out. But this was the artist's imagination so he decided to create something that made no sense, something no one would get, and put it in the main hall on the ship.

Floyd and Benny looked at it for quite some time as it fascinated them. They stood there nearly over ten minutes (which was saying something).

"Who would you think would want to put this over here?" Floyd asked curiously.

"Dunno," Benny replied as he looked at every detail. Benny always had the master taste for art, lectures, pomes, drama, and everything else that was like that. He was a good at figuring out what really suited him and what didn't; but this was hard for him to make out.

"I imagine that he might've been a dolphin once," Benny theorised about the sculptor's story.

"Really?" Floyd asked as he stared at Benny.

"I think he was some dude once, till people did something wrong to him, and he started to plan to take over the galaxy or something." Benny continued, "I imagine that he built a legion and started to conquer. He brought a bag of mythical and legendary feathers to aid him in his conquest, then finds a mysterious apple which could empower him with a single thought!"

They stood there for a couple of moments until Floyd thought to change the subject.

"Do you know where Lilly and Alex are?"

"No," Benny acknowledged, as he was in deep thought. "If I had Alex's lazy thoughts and Lilly's mastery skills, I could pinpoint where they are without trying to go and find them."

"Do you have that ability?" Floyd asked, unsure of Benny's methods.

Benny said nothing as he was focussing. "No."

"Hmm," Floyd said as he walked over to the ship's map and told Benny, "they could be waiting for us in the dining hall."

"Why you think that?" Benny asked.

"If I had to go somewhere to quiet down without getting involved in any places that screamed at you with colour and glummer, I would go there."

Benny felt disappointed as it seemed like the sort of place he would've gone as well. He and Floyd walked like slow joggers and the sculpture was left alone. It grew sad that no one else gave it any complements.

8. Being Boarded is Never a Good Sign

Outside in space, not too far away from the La-Gold, a savage pirate cruiser was heading to the cruise ship. They had picked up a signal which gave them word that all the ship's security's system was down and was vulnerable, meaning more bounty ahead!

These were thugs and thieves from many different parts of the galaxy. People who, if they heard of a place full of glorious money that was up for grabs, would head right to it.

Overall, this was a mission. A spy within the cruise ship gave them the order that it was all clear. They couldn't wait to see what they could steal. Like the saying went: it was the finest cruise ship in the galaxy!

Lilly and Alex sat around a table with white sheets on it. The chamber was large enough but not as massive as a dining room. There were other tables with guests eating marvellous food and waiters/waitresses giving out their orders.

Lilly felt awkward as they sat, like they were having the strangest dinner in their lifetime. Alex was meddling with his hands while Lilly was bored out of her brain.

"How could you pay for all of this?" Lilly asked Alex. She knew this was something they couldn't get out of quite so easily.

"We always get out of messes like this," Alex told her quite relaxed. "We'll just head off and won't talk about it."

"Not always," Lilly said seriously. "This is money, 'Real' money!"

"Money or no money," Alex said as he sat straight, "we've done so much stuff like this before, and we've done worse than not paying for something, why is this so different?"

"Because I have a small feeling that our holiday here might come to an abrupt end, much sooner than you expect." Lilly whispered until Benny and Floyd landed in their seats. Lilly changed the subjected while giving out a fake smile.

"Sorry we're late," Benny said.

"We forgot the memo," Floyd mentioned, as he remembered somewhere in his brain to meet the others here.

"We didn't get a memo," Benny told him.

"Oh," Floyd said, surprised. "Well, the important thing is we've found you."

They sat there for a few seconds as Floyd and Benny caught their breaths after their exciting exploration. Meanwhile, Floyd and Alex shared glances as something must have got their attention. Floyd didn't know what, but Alex did.

"You sure you know where we're going, or are you following your instincts?" Alex questioned the librarian on the spot.

Floyd gave a blank expression as he replied, "No, remember, this is the impossible we're finding here. It doesn't pop out, out of nowhere. But if we keep going, moving from planet to planet, there will still be a chance of finding it."

They sat there in silence. When Floyd's drink arrived and he held it before he drank, Lilly commented, "A chance?!"

"That's like a glimmer of succeeding," Benny said, doubtful.

"Okay, let's not get too carried away with ourselves," Floyd told them.

"You really don't know where we're going, do you?!" Alex asked him.

"I do," the librarian lied, as he didn't have that much knowledge yet. "If I haven't…", he stopped, putting his glass down. "Okay, I've heard that there will be one of a few planets over in the south-west, where there is a gateway of galaxies into more galaxies."

"Are you serious?" Lilly said, unimpressed.

"The myth?" Alex thought before he could chuckle.

"It isn't a myth," Floyd told them seriously, "I know in my heart that it's out there. You lot said you needed my help so that's why I dropped everything to do so."

"Then…you've been helping this whole time?" Benny said as the Mercent Siblings started to feel guilty for mistreating Floyd.

Before Floyd could keep speaking, someone picked him up out of his seat. An arm crossed his shoulders and put his other hand over Floyd's mouth.

Another person stepped in front of Floyd and turned towards the Mercent Siblings.

"PARDON ME, EVERYONE", said LO-NO with a hysterical laugh while the siblings stared with confusion. "MY FRIEND HERE HAS BEEN AVOIDING SOME VERY IMPORTANT DUTIES WHICH HE CANNOT ESCAPE FROM, AND WE'RE HERE TO COLLECT HIM FROM HIS OUTRAGEOUS ADVENTURE!"

"HIS DISTNATION HAS REACHED THE END," YO-NO commented.

"Oh, wait a sec!" Floyd spoke as he pushed YO-NO away. "I haven't avoided anything!"

"OH YES YOU DID!" LO-NO told him directly that he wasn't going to take anymore nonsense from the librarian. "YOU STOLE OFF WHILE WE'VE BEEN LOOKING UP AND DOWN TO FIND YOU! I

IMAGINE THAT THE LIBRARY HAS BEEN UNGUARDED FOR ABOUT FIVE DAYS NOW, WITH NO ONE LOOKING AFTER IT!"

"How many times do I have to say this?" Floyd told them, annoyed. "I am going to go back to the library."

"BUT WHY DIDN'T YOU COME SOONER?" LO-NO asked. "WHY HAVEN'T YOU TOLD ME WHAT PLANS YOU WERE GOING TO HAVE WHILE I WAS SHUT DOWN?"

"It's just there's so much to discover here," Floyd told him, "And also the time stream is clunky. But I will have time to fix it all, promise."

Then, LO-NO's patience ran out.

"OK! YOU'VE GONE FAR ENOUGH," he said, unfolding his arms as if he pretended he had sleeves. YO-NO stopped him in his tracks as he tried to pull him back.

"LET ME HAVE HIM!!!" LO-NO roared.

"VIOLENCE IS NOT THE RIGHT SOLUTION," YO-NO told his robotic brother.

"I DON'T CARE! HIS LOAN HAS EXPIRED!"

Then, as Floyd leapt, a massive explosion blasted from the entrance to the room up the stairs where at the door came pirates carrying heavy weapons and knives.

"OK!" said one of them who smirked greedily, "Hand over and deliver! And try not to call security!"

Floyd was just standing there as everyone froze, but LO-NO and YO-NO's whereabouts became a mystery. Floyd turned to face the Mercent Siblings, but they were also gone. Until a hand picked out his robe when he saw they were under the table.

Floyd joined them as they were trying to not be noticed.

"OK," Lilly said quietly, "we have to get past those pirates without them seeing us."

"Unnoticed," Benny replied nervous. "Great."

"We're never quite the best at that," Alex commented.

"We don't get a vote in this!" Lilly told her brother angrily. "We need to get out and fast!"

"Why do I have a bad feeling this ship is going to have a bad ending," Floyd thought to himself, but all the siblings heard him which they thought wasn't helping.

Benny popped his head out of the table and saw the guests giving the pirates all their belongings. Then he saw that the entrance was unattended, so this was the perfect opportunity.

He looked back down to his gang as he gave them the all-clear sign. Floyd had no idea what it meant but he followed their lead.

They crept through the entrance as they crouched down. After they got out of the room, that was only the first part of fifty of their problems solved right now; the other problems were to get off the ship.

Captain Benison was at the control room as he watched the pirates taking control of his ship through the many screens around him. It seemed everything was going haplessly; the guests were frightened and stood put, while the crew planned to evacuate into the escape pods with many of the guests as soon as possible.

While the captain was staying put, he was hoping that his butler would come and tell him about how this nonsense happened.

"Union!!!", he shouted through the speakers as load as he could. But he had been calling for him for the last few minutes out of his lungs. "Where is that pitiful butler?"

Then, there was a sound dazzling through another sound which kept Benison straight.

"Union? Is that you?"

Then a voice came in.

"Yes sir," it replied. It was Union, which relieved the captain.

"Have you seen what happened? They have taken over the ship! What kept you?"

The butler went into silence for a moment.

"Ah, sorry, sir," the butler spoke nervously. "I had to assist the new passenger; well, the one that was making the big fuss."

"You looked after it?' the captain asked.

"Yes sir," the butler confirmed. "I was taking him to his room, until these pirates came and invaded the place." Then, the butler went silent again. "Well, I wouldn't want to go into more detail about what our guest did to them."

As much the captain would have loved to hear Union's progress, the captain felt trapped among the crew and passengers. The guests and everyone else had no way out other than being robbed. The captain's options were limited except for one.

"Union, I you need to you to escort the guests off the ship and get out safely," the captain ordered.

"Sir," Union said, as he may have understood what the captain was doing, "are you going to do it?"

"It leaves me with no other option," the captain said. "Union, you are dismissed from further duties."

"Thank you, sir," Union replied as he vanished.

The Captain went over to the control panel and started to press on the keyboard. He called out, "Computer, set to self-destruct in ten minutes."

He wasn't the most common of captains, or at least not of the ones who died trying. He didn't have any plan or any other way that he and his crew could escape. But he shall be remembered as the captain who piloted the finest cruise ship in the galaxy.

Floyd and his friends marched over to the escape pods which were stacked in line while an alarm flashed red, and a computer voice told them to hurry up or be blown to bits.

"Man, why didn't the captain give more of a heads up?!" Benny complained nervously.

"Who cares!" Alex told him. "The only thing that matters is that we get out of here."

By now, a bunch of the crew had already arrived in the bay. A maximum of six people could enter each pod as the door shields went up and the pods bunked down into the stars.

While Floyd was figuring out the password to open the pod's door, Benny turned his head as the Ratan jumped into his face in a flash, letting out a terrifying roar. Benny leapt back frightened as Union took the creature and rushed along.

"Sorry about that," Union said to Benny as he led the creature to the nearest pod. He opened the pod's door and left the Ratan in there. "Please do find any free meals wherever you go." He farewelled the Ratan as it stared back at the butler.

But before the creature could reply, the pod's door flew up and the pod dropped down with speed.

"Phew, at least we got that done," Union said in relief as he started to rush to the nearest pod.

Then Floyd finally got his pod's door to open.

"Got it!" he shouted as he and the Mercent Siblings entered. The whole place was clean and clear with a white and blue wall curved in a spiral.

They sat in the cosy seats and strapped themselves in with seatbelts. Lilly was in front of the control panel.

"Quite cosy," Floyd said, to which no one replied. "No? No one?"

"And I thought I was enjoying myself," Benny said sadly as Floyd gave him a pat on the back.

"I think we all did," Lilly added as she also felt a bit disappointed as well, "but I promise you, Benny, we'll all go on an amazing vacation after we get out of here…"

But as Lilly finished her sentence, she accidently pressed a button and the pod's door closed up and made the pod fly down, firing its engines as it headed towards one of the nearest planets.

9.   The True Faces

There were about five nearest habitable planets that the pods were heading toward. One was called J-cooler, which was a massive snowy planet that was made entirely of water, but if the passengers were lucky, they may be able to meet the snow-gins. There were also the woods of Scholia, the pink world of Scapula, and the sealess ocean world Limnos. But there was also the deserted desert Riminess, which wasn't any tourist top destination, but it was, however, where the pod that Floyd and the Mercent Siblings were in was heading toward.

There weren't many records about this planet because nobody visited it. But if you do make your way there, be warned: it has extreme sandstorms that appeared every seventy-two hours, and it was not rare to see one each ten minutes.

The pod crashed into the sand dunes, which formed a narrow landscape that was the same height level. They noticed that the communications weren't working because of the interference of the sandstorm.

"Why does it have to be Riminess," Lilly moaned.

Lilly flicked buttons as she hoped something may appear; Floyd scanned the screens as he thought he could assist.

"I'll take it that help isn't going to come?" he asked quite bleak.

"Nothing's working. I can't even move out of this mud," she said as the light was dimming down.

All they could see in their mirror was sand and darkness, which was giving them some bad signs.

"By what I can see is we're going underneath the sand," Floyd mentioned as it should be of some importance to the group.

"Yeah, we can see that," Lilly told him.

"I think it's a better idea if we try getting out of here," Benny said.

"I don't think we're going anywhere soon", Lilly broke the news. "The engines are stuck by the pressure of the sand and the door is jammed."

"Then we're stuck?!" Benny thought, overacting.

"No, I think we should at least try to get out of this dump before we die in here," Alex suggested.

They went over to the pod's door and tried to budge it open. They hit, wracked and slammed it but with only a few effects.

Then as her brothers opened the pod's door, sand poured down, and everyone watched in horror.

"Get out!" Lilly ordered as they rushed towards the door and tried to pull themselves out.

The sand was rather difficult to get through as they had to push themselves out of it with enough pressure.

"Auruuughhhh!!!" Alex called as he tried to reach the tip of the door, "it's harder to do that!!!!"

"We've been in worse situations than this!!!" Lilly told them, as she knew they had the confidence to get free.

They pushed through but only three managed to get out of the intense wave of sand. Benny was still stuck on the other side.

Alex grabbed Benny's hand from the other side as Benny had difficulty swimming through sand.

"Come on!" Alex told Benny confidently. "I'll get you out as much as I can!"

"Don't let the sand eat me!" Benny worried as the sand was building up inside of the pod.

Then Alex pulled Benny out. They leapt out of the pod and rolled over down through the dunes.

Floyd and Lilly watched as the brothers were rolling on each other.

"Oh, brother," Lilly sighed in disgust.

Then as Floyd and Lilly chased after Alex and Benny, Floyd noticed through the terrible vision that the storm was blocking, what appeared to be a monument that was made of copestone. It caught the librarian's attention as the sand flicked into his eyes.

"Ow!" he commented, as he headed down to check the thing out more clearly. He appeared at the monument, and the Mercent Siblings weren't too far away to observe.

But something that Floyd didn't spot was a lean and stretchy coffin in front of the monument. There were five bricked pillars surrounding the area. Each of them had different symbols and each pillar was coloured differently: orange, brown-like orange, violet, deep red, and bright yellow. They stared at the coffin and studied the pillars.

"Is this someone's funeral that we've intruded on?" Benny asked, quite embarrassed. "I don't want to disrespect the dead by being here."

"I don't think it's a funeral, Benny," Alex told his brother to not feel bad.

Floyd looked over the area as he tried to get a good view of the desert, but it appeared he couldn't see much more than thirty feet.

"Uh," Floyd could only say as he couldn't see anything useful nearby.

But not far away, which they did not know, was a group of purple masked creatures who ducked under the sand or were near to one of their tombs. They saw their unwelcome visitors to the ceremony.

You may think that no life would survive in these conditions, but their blood was stable in this environment, plus they could see through the storm very easily. The growled in anger as they planned to ambush the humans.

But while the humans waited for any representation, a moving figure was seen through the storm. It was leany and was humanoid in shape.

"Hey, look," Alex told the others who also noticed. "Hello!"

Then came the butler Union who still had his gun in his hand, which he pointed at them.

"You really think you would have been all alone?" the butler asked. His voice changed rapidly as he wasn't the sort of person who would have helped anyone: he was a spy!

He had joined the La-Gold Cruise to only let the pirates raid the ship, and this was a task given to him by a rich crime lord.

"So", he said with a greedy smirk, "I want all of you to shut up as my pickup will arrive shortly."

"Yay!" Benny celebrated. "We're saved!"

"I said shut up!" the butler ordered as he pointed his gun directly at Benny who held up his arms.

"Okay, okay…," Floyd told the butler, "maybe we could make an agreement, you and I…"

"What?!" the butler blushed. "You really think you could persuade me? I'm getting lots of money because of this. 'A lot' of money in fact."

Floyd gave a blank face. "Maybe I can't guarantee you on that, but can't you at least leave me and my friends in peace?'

But the butler was growing very impatient with the librarian. Just then a spear was tossed and nearly hit Alex.

"Hey!" Alex called annoyed. "Whoever threw that, I want to hear an explanation!"

Then sounds of whispers of the alien locals swerved through the sand. The aliens came closer to them and soon they were surrounded: the humans were crowed with nowhere to go.

"Why are they doing that?" Alex asked a bit frightened. His siblings and Floyd stuck together closely.

"If you ask nicely, maybe they might tell you?" Floyd replied, unsure.

"I won't have this!" the butler called out. "Time is precious, and so is my payment."

Then, without noticing, Lilly wacked Union with a staff and he dropped down on the ground. Floyd and the others were stunned at what they witnessed, and Lilly turned back to them and asked, "What? Never had any dealings with jerks and putting them in their place?"

"Uh, not like that," Floyd responded. "But I mean, wow! That was totally incredible!"

"You really have to see us in action", Benny told Floyd.

"But can someone focus on the now?!" Alex reminded them tensely. "We still have trouble on our backs!"

"I wouldn't worry, Alex," Lilly commented.

A flash of white light surrounded them as it scared away the alien tribe who hid through the sandstorm. As it came into closer view, they noticed that it was a small ship and it spotted them.

"I think we got it covered," Lilly added.

After the ship rescued Floyd and the Mercent Siblings, as they left Riminess, they had many stops on the way. First, they had to go to the Alito Police Space Station to drop Union off.

Then the ship made a pit stop to Vexas where Floyd and the Mercent Siblings had an awful feeling that their rescuers were getting suspicious and might do something bad to them.

They hitched a ride on an abandoned ship while the rescuers were getting ship gear from the wreckage. Then they passed through the inside of the Maxime System and passed over small planets that had some strong gravitational pulls that was drawing them in.

Then, not far away from the Maxime System, they landed on the tall hilly highland isles of Marland, which was full of a massive ocean with a town of buildings at the dock side of the islands.

Floyd and the siblings relaxed at a bar as they planned the next step of their journey. Benny and Alex were having a laugh together until they spotted an old friend of theirs from their past.

"Oh God," Benny spoke horrified.

"What?' Alex asked with a frown.

"Five o'clock," Benny warned as he tried to move his face away. "You can't miss him."

Alex did look where Benny told him and what Alex saw was a picky and large alien that was wandering through the place. His species was some kind of fish-like sea serpent but was green. He was accompanied by a large number of friends he was chatting to as they cheered.

"Oh God," Alex responded. He also tried to look at the other way, then looked back at Benny and whispered, "try chatting with each other like normal and try not to make any attention to draw you to you-know-who."

They laughed together for a moment, while Floyd was aiding Lilly to a component on their newest ship.

"Screwdriver," Lilly asked, and Floyd gave her quite a fancy tool which she twisted onto the device.

"Tape."

Floyd gave Lilly the tape as she shielded off an open part of the device.

"Repair gun."

"I thought we didn't have any of those?" Floyd asked as he shortly found one under the table and gave it to her.

Lilly finished repairing and the device was as good as new. She sprung it around with a smile, then slammed it onto the table. She looked at Benny and Alex who gave a sign of worry.

"What's wrong?"

"Ox Jaddo is here," Alex warned.

"What?!" Lilly said in shock, then noticed that Floyd was between them. She crouched over and whispered to her brothers, "We need to leave as soon as possible after we're done here!"

"Wait, what is this all about?" Floyd asked who had a fumbling feeling that something wasn't right.

Alex looked at Floyd and then stared at his siblings. They were thinking that the truth should come out, but they gave a couple of glances before discussing the issue.

"Stop doing that!" Floyd said. He was observing, and the signs they gave worried him. "What is it?"

Then, they all gave a sheepish expression as Lilly turned towards the librarian, "Floyd, we haven't been completely honest with you…"

"We're thieves," Benny moaned. Lilly and Alex dropped an unimpressed look in his direction.

"Oh," Floyd replied as he sat there for several moments trying to get all the details right into his head. Then he started to act disbelieving.

"Wait, hold on. You're saying I've been hanging out with criminals?!"

"We're not criminals," Alex corrected him, "we only cause a small portion of crime."

"But, but, why?!"

"We wanted to explore the galaxy," Benny told his friend, "we get into some…misfitful things along the way, but we're good! honest!"

"And you would have me believe that I could trust you?!"

"We're better people than you know," Lilly said as she tried to win Floyd's trust back. "We're sorry that we haven't told you earlier; we knew that at one point on our adventure you might act this way."

"Well, you have that right", the Librarian called harshly. He needed a breath of air, and to isolate himself from them. He got up and left the bar.

The siblings grew an ugly feeling in their gut for the first time.

Then Lilly had to ask, "Did we do the right thing?"

"He'll get used to it," Alex poured a drink for himself and sipped.

"But Floyd was like the closest friend that I ever had," Benny said, quite sad.

"Hold on!" Alex added, "you really think he is going to stick around with us? Even when he knows the truth and what we're capable of?"

"Alex!" Lilly snapped. "We can't just keep doing this, alright?! Maybe you can, but I'm not giving up on Floyd!"

Lilly took off and left the bar, and shortly after Benny followed her as well.

10. The Tables have Turned

While the Siblings were feeling horrible, they were trying to figure out a way to apologise to Floyd, which wasn't an easy fix. Floyd went back to their ship in disapproval, which was quite hard for the siblings to handle.

The librarian isolated himself in his own quarters of the ship, as the ship itself was large enough to carry a crew of seven in total. As much as Alex wasn't affected by this, it troubled both Benny and Lilly who thought they should talk privately in the long corridor. They had grown so close to Floyd in the last few days, which wasn't a friendship they thought they would have.

"What are we going to do, Benny?" Lilly asked her brother for help.

"I don't know!" Benny moaned cluelessly.

"That's not helping!"

"I know, sorry," Benny apologised. "It's just that I don't want to lose our friend who we've been getting along with so well."

"And isn't someone who wanted to kill us - and who doesn't want to go for Alex," Lilly thought as she tried to come up with some ideas. "But what should we do?"

They were trying to think of options, until Benny thought of one. "OK," he said, "he has been our best and only friend we ever had."

"Yeah, and?"

"We should do something, something he wants us to do, which can win his trust in us again."

"I actually like that idea," Lilly told Benny. "but he is likely to hitch a ride out of here sooner rather than later, so we have to do it before then."

"I know, but what can we offer?"

Lilly froze then thought, "We stay out of trouble."

"Ah, that will be hard to do," Benny responded, "trouble is part of our last name."

"Then we won't steal anything anymore."

"Really?" Benny said a bit sad. "Not even the smallest briskets?"

"Benny, this is more important than our despicable traits!" Lilly said as she tried not to get angry. "This is about Floyd. If we are ever going to make proper friends again, we have to give up what we do so we keep those relationships."

Benny was trying to hold back his emotions inside as thievery was something that they always did. But he wondered, "What about Alex?"

Lilly gave an empty expression, then added, "Forget about Alex," she said, "this is about us, and what we can do moving forward."

As this meeting came to a successful conclusion, they headed back to the piloting room. As they arrived, they saw the area glowed with green tiles and the walls were painted with blue circle patterns.

Floyd was drinking his coke as he admired the stars through the wide windows' yellow glass. Alex was busy driving as he set the coordinates for their next destination.

Lilly and Benny sat not too far away from Alex. Floyd sat over in the corner, and tried not to make any eye contact, which was really awkward.

"Well," Benny spoke, "I hope you will stay with us a little longer."

Floyd didn't comment but slurped.

"Alright, alright," Benny continued, "maybe we can invite you to this amazing royal plaza that we know offers the best hot chocolate in the galaxy."

The librarian said nothing for the moment; he later gave a disappointing glance as he got up. He knew if he kept tagging along with them, he would likely be caught in a massive chase across the stars by a fleet who would hunt them down and send them to galactic prison. That was not what Floyd wanted.

Then, Alex noticed something right ahead of them which drew him to worry.

"Uh-oh," he said which caught everyone's attention, including Floyd, who stopped and turned around. What they all saw was an asteroid field they were about to enter.

"Alex," Lilly told her brother, a bit shaken, "get us out of here!"

"WATCH OUT!!!" Benny told his brother as he saw a large boulder coming right at them.

Alex moved the ship out of the boulder's direction, but multiple rocks were coming at them all at once.

The ship ducked down and spun out of the way as the asteroids clashed into each other in a slam as pieces scattered into stardust. The pieces of destroyed rocks did eventually hit parts of the ship, including a crack in one of the windows, which Benny watched in horror.

The ship sped up as every time the ship found a big rock, there always appeared to be more waiting on the other side coming towards it. It was like you only had five seconds to get out of every encounter or you were dead.

The crew shortly became ill from Alex's wild piloting skills, which surprisingly was keeping them alive.

"Lilly, I need you to take over!" Alex said, quite overloaded.

"Keep your eyes on flying!" Lilly told him to focus.

"But I'm really sick and I don't think my guts can take any more of this!"

Benny raced down to the toilets and Floyd just stood there as he wasn't sure what he could do.

"Uh…," he responded as he spung around and tried to gather thoughts in his brain, "uh…"

Then to their horror - with their jaws dropped - they saw right ahead of them was a gigantic rock that was nearly a size of a thirty-storey building. There was nowhere to escape, except Alex found a large hole which he thought their ship could fit through.

He flew straight towards it as his sister outburst, "WHAT ARE YOU DOING?!"

"I got this," he said, nearly chilled.

The ship parked into the hole, hovering; but the massive rock moved about, so they waited until they got a chance to exit through a clear space.

When they did, the ship zoomed out as more rocks headed towards them, but smaller and coming faster. Lilly noticed that Alex had enough as he collapsed at the controls. Lilly quickly grabbed the lever as the ship tossed around and a few rocks hit and damaged parts of the ship.

Benny made his way back into the room as he saw his brother laying on the floor.

"Benny!" Lilly ordered him, "I need you to take Alex and put him somewhere to not drawl on my boots. Floyd! I may need some piloting assistance!"

Floyd gave a massive blank and nervous expression as he froze, "Uhh…"

"Hurry!" Lilly told him. Floyd got a move on and sat on the seat next to her as he got a closer view of the mayhem unfolding.

"Now, where should we go?" Lilly asked Floyd.

Floyd's brain was in no condition to handle the stress he was feeling. He could only see rocks of all sizes in every direction. But he noticed from above, not that far away, a wide rocky surface.

"There!" he directed.

"I see it!" Lilly said as she swung the ship up to miss another row of collapsing rocks. But as they reached upward, they came into a section of the area where the rocky walls were starting to collide into each other.

"Oh God, its closing!" Lilly replied, as she noticed she needed a lot more height to get through. She sped up in maxim speed as parts of the wall started to clash as dust flunked and tiny rocks deflected the ship.

Everyone was bracing for impact, but Lilly kept going till she was able to get the ship out as the walls finally clashed into a connected surface.

They were in a safe area where they could see the asteroid field surrounding a few gigantic asteroids that had an empty river leading them through the rocks.

As everyone was calming down, Benny was relieved that he had survived for another day. Floyd was happy that he helped out, and Alex was gasping for air after almost dying. Lilly felt she came first place rather than second.

As Alex was able to function properly, he replied to Lilly, "Sis, thank you."

"You're welcome," Lilly commented with a smile.

"That was so close," Benny said as he could hardly believe that they were still alive.

"I don't think I've been in any worse situation than that," Floyd acknowledged, but he had to agree with Benny, that it was only just rare luck they were alive.

As they continued to follow the empty trail, they found themselves in a space dome that was connected to the surface. Inside the dome, they could see a big white citadel.

"Is it just me, or is everyone seeing this?' Floyd asked the siblings.

11. The Citadel in the Middle of the Asteroids

The Narre-Seven flew above the mysterious dome citadel that had three overly large towers peeking out. Everyone took a closer view at it to check they weren't dreaming.

"Wow!" Benny said astonished. "I didn't know someone could live all the way out here."

"I don't think anyone can," Lilly thought clearly, as it would seem impossible for anyone to make it out here.

"I wonder who must have made this," Floyd wondered curiously. "Where do they get the materials to build here? How is it possible that this is here?"

Alex paid much attention to the construction of the citadel. It was polished and quite new, which seemed to put him off edge. Then he looked at the scan radar on the ship.

"It looks like someone is inviting us to go in."

With everyone happily agreeing to get a proper look, the Narre-Seven flew down towards the landing bay that was in a small hatch and had a massive red line that was leading them to an open round tunnel leading them in.

After the ship landed in the docking bay, they started to walk through the corridor that would lead them right into the entry of the capital. The floor had a long red carpet and there were see-through glass walls that cycled over them. They could see space and the asteroid surface quite clearly through it.

They were quite surprised that whoever invented all of this must have gone to all the trouble of making it.

"Who you think made this?" Benny asked everyone.

"Someone with a lot of money, I imagine," Alex pointed out.

It looked like this place seemed to be still in the making. Everything so far just seemed so clean with no displays or any funky decorations.

"I wonder if anyone is out here?" Floyd pondered.

"If there was anyone, I do hope they have good service," Alex commented.

On the other side of that corridor, coming in light speed toward them was, uh-oh, a robot which shivered Floyd's mind. Its legs were a whole wheel at the bottom of a sharp and shiny blue body. It had normal sized arms but were thin, and same went for the round grey head, with its yellow eyes.

It didn't say a word to its visitors as they looked at it quite unsure.

"Umm…," Benny said, "Hi, little buddy? Are you still active and all that?"

Then coming out behind the, oh-no, robot was a blue holographic woman, which you could easily tell was digital by all the patterns that was showing on her. She had long hair coming down to her shoulders and she also had sparkly jewellery. She wore a glittery dress that was so shiny that the designer worked a lot of detail into it.

She was projected by the little robot, and it appeared that she was the only thing it was casting.

"Why, hello", she said, quite normally, as she looked at each visitor. *"Welcome to Venetian!"*

To Floyd and the Mercent Sibling, it appeared that she wasn't a recorded hologram. It appeared that she was functionally normal as she was controlling her programming.

"We weren't expecting to have any visitors quite so soon," she said quite surprised. *"Who are you?"*

Floyd and the siblings shared glances as they weren't sure what to say.

"Sorry if we're intruding, but we only came here by accident," Floyd explained. "We were in the middle of the asteroid field, and we only just managed to arrive here."

"That makes logical sense," the woman added. *"Then, you can stay as long as you like. We have plenty of entertainment, refreshments, hospitality, anything you could imagine."*

"What is this place, if I may ask?" Lilly asked the woman.

"This was once our inventor's prime city. He planned to create it to bring a beacon for people to live and experience his new civilisation, but after years of building and creating us, his life was tragically cut short and the rest of us don't know how to proceed other than being empty machines."

"With power still on?" Floyd asked. "What kept you going? What sort of energy system are you harnessing?'

"Our inventor left an ongoing source for us as if he did pass on, we would still keep the place up and running so everything wouldn't shut down onto itself." she said as the bot led them through the corridor and journeyed towards the entrance.

They finally arrived in the main hall chamber that was quite tall, where they could see balconies to different floors throughout the citadel. The lighting was gashing so that everything seemed to have a nice feel all of a sudden. There were also doorways and stairs leading into different parts of the citadel, which they thought made everything feel like an art gallery.

The little robots moved in different parts of the citadel as they weren't affected by the visitors.

"What our inventor planned for us was to welcome visitors and make them feel right at home."

Everyone was studying the whole area. Alex was left questioning, "Since when was this whole construct built?"

"About 85 years ago," the woman replied. *"Our inventor died about three years later, and we were only left to our own isolation."*

"So, let me get this straight," Floyd added up, "you all have been around functioning for eighty years, and you haven't seen a single living being since then?"

The woman nodded as the librarian turned to figure out all the details. He couldn't think of any technology that would be still active for such a long time with no one observing. Even Floyd's NO bots have something that always keeping them functioning.

"Huh," he could only say as he was in deep thought.

"Hey lady!" Benny went up front. "Is there like any buffets here?"

"We can easily arrange for one of our bots to set up meals in the dining room," the lady responded. *"Anyway, the bots will lead you to wherever you want to go. When you're at Venetian, we'll be serving the best we can so you all can have a marvellous time."*

"Okay, yeah, can someone take me somewhere where I can have a massage?" Alex asked as one of the little bots led him in a different direction, while everyone else went on different paths; except Lilly, who was standing in the main hall.

The holographic woman disappeared as Lilly was starting to grow suspicious about Venetian.

The bots took the party to the places where they wanted to go. Alex went into a yoga room as he did couple of exercises while the bots were set in fan mode and a gash of wind blew in his direction. At the right moment, they asked him if he wanted a milk shake.

Benny was drinking and eating a bunch of food in the dining room. Shortly he headed to a club room where he was competing in a table tennis match with one of bots.

And as for Floyd, he got himself some briskets to keep him occupied as he walked around the citadel to observe the construction and hopefully know more about it. He soon walked back to the round glass corridor near to the landing bay and he spotted Lilly snooping.

For the first time in her life, Lilly felt more like an investigator than a thief. She knew right to her nose that something wasn't right. All the pieces were jumbled about and were not making sense.

"Ah! I can see that you've found something that caught your attention," Floyd spotted as he walked up to her.

She was kneeling down as she studied the floor, how it appeared so clean that there wasn't a footprint on it other than theirs. Then she noticed that there was no display, no welcoming sign, nothing.

"Floyd, I'm telling you, something's not right here," she responded back to the librarian as she got up.

"I've been thinking the same thing," he said as it was troubling him too. "The whole story about how they were still able to be activated for a couple of decades and there wasn't anyone who was supervising them this whole time."

"I know, right?" Lilly though the exact same thing which scared her. Then she thought to change the subject. "I was going to talk to you, about us."

"Ah", Floyd said, as he knew what she was talking about. "Don't worry about it."

Lilly froze as this wasn't a reaction she was expecting. "You're sure?"

"Yeah," Floyd said, relaxed. "I know people do things that are quite stupid, which is what everybody does. But I shouldn't judge what people do by their actions, its who they are."

"Nononononono!" Lilly stopped Floyd. "I wanted to make it up to you."

"You don't have to; nobody does that to me."

"But me and Benny made a deal to never do thievery ever again."

"And Alex?"

"He wouldn't comply," Lilly knew inside and out. Then she looked quite relieved. "So you're cool with us?"

"Yeah, it's something for me to adjust to but I'll easily keep up."

Then, Lilly was focussed back on the Capital, as she thought she would tell Floyd about the dangers. "But really, I've got a real bad feeling about being here. Could you at least ponder about the place a little bit more and try not to give out information to my brothers?"

"Will do," Floyd promised Lilly, as he turned around and headed back to the Capital. Lilly kept investigating the area.

Little did they know that they weren't alone.

12. Tension Rising

Floyd wandered across a couple of hallways and stairs and reached another big hall with more bots, where he could see a glass roof right above him. The weird thing Floyd noticed as he entered the room, was that the bots were starting to watch him as the librarian tried to act normal. One bot bumped into him by accident which made Floyd jump; then the hologram of the woman appeared from its projector.

"*Ah, Floyd, was it?* she asked.

"Ah, yes," the librarian confirmed. "Do you have a name? or a number?"

"*I'm VAH. I was wondering if you are lost?*"

"Lost?" Floyd said, startled. "No, I was just looking at the beautiful place. I do love to see what a big tower has to offer."

VAH gave Floyd a narrow look.

"*I don't want you to go much further,*" she warned.

"Can't I?" Floyd asked. It seemed he must have triggered something for her to question him. The bots made a sizzling sound at him; Floyd didn't have a clue what they were doing, but he knew VAH wanted him to keep away from what she was doing.

"You know what, I think I'll do what you say", Floyd replied with a smile, as he tried not to show any fear.

The bots stopped the noise as VAH returned a smile back, *"Your friends are waiting for you at our waiting room."*

"Really?" Floyd replied back. One of the bots started to lead him. "That's nice. I always wanted friends to wait for me," he said, as he went off into one of the corridors as the hologram woman disappeared.

At this moment, Floyd felt things were getting out of hand and fast. He thought VAH was right onto him, and he didn't know how long he and the Mercent Siblings had until things got nasty.

He quickly shut off the bot he was with and stuffed him inside one of the nearest closets and started to run. Floyd headed through different parts of the Capital until he spotted some of the small bots in the distance. Then he tried to withdraw his steps backward.

Floyd went everywhere to search for the siblings, but he had no sign of them. It appeared that the place had become quieter than before, which made Floyd panic.

He continued his search as he walked down one of the narrow corridors and soon spotted a room that had a sign that said, "SUBJECT TESTING G-5 IN PROGRESS". The door was open that led to a dark chamber inside. Floyd had a terrible feeling that he should go in.

Floyd entered inside. The room was all black and he saw the Mercent Siblings unconscious and strapped on separate operating tables. And there was a mechanical moving robot attached to the roof that had many arms with different tools as it was testing them. The siblings also had small dots on their foreheads as one of the robot arms pointed a small red laser at them. Three screens popped up which showed their heart beats and their cells.

"Hey, you!", Floyd called out, cowardly and stupidly afterwards.

The machine turned its head and looked at him.

"WHO ARE YOU?" it said as its voice took up the whole room.

"I…I have better questions for you!" Floyd said. "Like, what have you got there?"

The robot moved one of its arms up and showed it to Floyd.

"THIS?" it said. "THIS WOULD KILL THE SUBJECT."

Floyd's throat glopped. "Well…so…I would tear it down," he said nervously.

"YOU WOULD LIKE THAT, WOULDN'T YOU?"

Floyd didn't decide to stay put. He raced over towards to the machine and jumped on its big body. It spung around with its arm moving as it tried to get Floyd off. Floyd stuck himself onto the body, as he gripped hold of it.

The machine slammed into the siblings as they fell out of their tables and began to wake up with confusion and saw Floyd facing off the machine. They were dizzy and their vision blurred as they couldn't respond properly.

Floyd started to climb up the machine trying to get to the top. It had little effect as its arm waved around trying to grab him. Floyd dropped down as one of its arms took his leg and pulled him down. Floyd held on as the arm pulled, and managed to open a hatch where wires of importance were stored. He pulled all the wires out as the arm threw Floyd on the ground and the machine started to crash.

"OH NO," it said, as it started to malfunction. "THAT'S THE PROBLEM BEING A ROBOTIC SURGEON, TOO MANY ARMS."

The machine soon stopped and shut down as Floyd caught his breath. Floyd later looked at the siblings who were now able to get up. He went over to them to give some support.

"We have to leave," Floyd told them. "VAH is going to find and kill us."

"That's always the problem with that sort of AI," Alex responded. "No matter what you think of it, they just want to kill you anyway."

Benny gave a sad expression once again, "And I thought I was enjoying myself."

"Come on", Lilly cheered Benny up. "We'll reach to our goal, after we get out of here alive."

"No, Benny's right," Floyd agreed sadly as well, "if this isn't a place where we could finally relax, I don't know what else has to offer anymore."

After they got out of the testing room, they headed back to the large hall at the entrance of the Capital, but as they arrived, the bots blocked their path and started to roll slowly towards them.

"Uh, hi guys!" Floyd said as he gave another nervous smile. The Mercent Siblings stood behind him. "We can sort something out, can't we?"

Then, with a startle, VAH appeared in the centre of the hall, but she was larger than before.

"We were this close on emulating your friends in secret, but no matter," VAH responded, *"we'll just have to do it here, where no one can intervene. You'll be dead in place like you're meant to be."*

Floyd and the siblings were shaking out of their bones as there was nowhere to go. The bots came closer. This might be the first time on their adventure that they're luck has run out. VAH had total control, and no one would ever know…

Then, BOOM!!!! A huge explosion hit the entrance which made VAH glitch as she was hardly able to control her appearance. Then the bots started to lose control. They were spinning around, hitting the wall and running away.

"WhAt iS T#is?!" she asked before she shut down.

Coming out of the entrance was band of space pirates, not the ones from the cruise but actual space pirates. They wore what a normal pirate normally wore if they were setting sail through the stars with their head bands and stuffy coats, and other daggy clothes. They came storming in as they swashed their swords and fired their canon blasters on the bots who scattered into pieces. They later journeyed through the citadel as they raided the place. Shame that what they found wouldn't be anything so interesting.

Coming out of the fog from the entrance was a pirate captain that had a long stuffy beard and a scarf, with a blue stuffed coat and a staff which was full of jewellery and treasure goodies glued on it. He also had small diamond buttons on the coat and wore rings that shone.

Benny's jaw dropped as he made a deep gasp, "Captain Lush!"

"Who?" Alex asked cluelessly.

Benny stared back at his brother quite shocked. "The most famous pirate captain who sailed through the Alstra stars, and discovered the Edin Whale before it went extinct?"

"Never heard of him," Alex commented.

Captain Lush looked at the people in front of him as he made an old-fashioned pirate laugh.

"Bring them on board!"

13. Auuuurrrrr!

When Lush said to bring them on board, it wasn't an invitation. Floyd and the siblings were forced to board a wooden ship that was much larger than the asteroids - about four hundred feet tall with a maximum of thirty docks.

The pilot room was the largest room which had massive windows that beamed the entire wall, so the captain knew where he was going while controlling his really big ship. He also had a wheel to steer in the centre, with no controls other than the control panels on either side of him which the crew was using.

Where Floyd and the siblings were taken was a storage room at one of the below decks, which was filled with boxes, crates, and rats. They were caught in a net that dangled few inches from the ground. They could hear crewmen talking from the other room.

"This is ridiculous!" Floyd complained, as he struggled to get out. "How could the captain treat us like this when he saved our skin?"

"So, this is how it goes then," Alex thought. "We relax for a little while till we have to save our lives, and after we get out of whatever situation we were in, we bump into more trouble. You see the cycle here?"

"Oh, give it a rest," Lilly told him, as he wasn't helping. "You're just fussed that there hasn't been a moment where you can keep to yourself."

"Because everything is distracting me!" Alex said in quite an outburst. "I just wanted to have a moment alone, finally be in peace and not worry…" Alex paused as he looked at Benny as he got out of the net with a knife in his hand. "Where did you get that?"

"I managed to pick-pocket one of the crew while they were taking us on board," Benny replied.

"Well, they say old habits don't come in handy," Lilly commented, as Benny cut open the net for everyone to get out.

They later looked around the room trying to find something to help them blend in. Floyd opened a chest that had pirate disguises. Benny brought another chest that had disguises too.

Floyd wore a pirate hat with a large cape that hid his ridiculous robe; the others worn other stuff that were very piratey and more suited to their style.

They all looked at themselves as Alex wondered, "Is this ever going to work?"

"There's so many of them here," Floyd told him quite relaxed. "They probably won't know who everyone is."

"Just act like them," Lilly said quite at ease.

"Oh, this is so fun you guys!" Benny said quite excited. "We're pirates!"

"Just for the meantime," Alex pointed out, as he didn't think he could get used to this get up all the time.

Floyd and the siblings got out of the storage room as none of the crew noticed they exited. They squeezed through the crew as it became very crowed. Lilly bumped into someone who was muscular and made a delightful, "Auuugghh!!!"

Lilly froze as she returned a, "Auuggghhh!!!"

Then Benny commented with an, "Auuuugggghhh!!!"

They looked at Floyd who turned around and gave an unsure, "Auugh?"

Alex gave them all a narrow and chill expression, as he responded, "How are you doing?"

While the pirates were drifting off onto whatever activity they were doing, Floyd and the siblings snuck away as they found a quieter spot to speak.

"Phew!" Benny called out in relief, "I wasn't sure how long I would be speaking like that."

"You say," Alex replied, as he felt this was less pleasant than he was expecting.

"Well, at least nobody recognised us," Lilly commented. "It's quite a good plan, if I have to say so myself."

Alex was bothered as he noticed an itchy scuff around his neck; he couldn't help himself but try to take it off.

Lilly grabbed his hand as she asked, "What are you doing?"

"I can't get used to dressing up", Alex said, quite bothered, "especially when we're wearing silly outfits."

Benny gasped, "Take that back!"

"No, I won't," Alex refused.

Floyd looked back and forth at them through his one eye while the other was covered by an eyepatch. He added, "Well, it did get us out, unnoticed."

"But wouldn't anyone know?" Alex whispered, "Will anyone go in and see if their prisoners are on the loose?"

They gave it deep thought until Floyd replied, "I don't think they would mind."

"Well, it's better if we go elsewhere on board so we can discuss where to go from here", Lilly said, as they made their way up the stairs.

As the pirate ship was coming closer to the edge of the universe, the savage pirate crew who invaded the La-Gold, spotted them drifting through the cosmos. The crew planned to raid Captain Lush's ship, as this would be the battle of the mightiest of pirates! There had been a munity as Union made his way back to them and was now captain. He wanted to take down this pirate ship and make Lush's reputation an insult to all pirate kind.

Union's crew went to the weaponry to gather weapons that were stashed, as they prepared to invade.

"Remember," Union said to his men, "we are here to show who we are! and to thank the man who has placed us here!"

"HAUURGH!!" they shouted.

"And because of him, we can all live our lives as we want. So, send in the catapults and take out the bridge!"

As they continued making way, they greeted more of the crew as they found another small spot where a round table was laid. Floyd and the Mercent Siblings plunked down on stools as Lilly took out a map that they found in the storage to make plans for the next step of their journey.

Benny was looking at the glittering view of the cosmos through the rounded window as it gave a nice sense of the scenery. Floyd and the others were discussing how to get off now as they planned ahead, while Benny wasn't listening.

But Benny spotted something out of the ordinary as he sees another ship, unlike theirs. This one was a proper spaceship, maybe half the size of Lush but it was coming their way.

"Hey, are we expecting to pick up a crew?" Benny asked.

"Uh, no", Lilly said as she was too busy focussing on talking with Floyd and Alex.

"Oh, it's just we're getting a large ship coming our way, who appears to be charging."

It stopped what the others were talking as they got up and looked at what Benny was talking about. They noticed that the ship was indeed coming at them in fast speed.

"GUYS, GET BACK!!!!!" Lilly said as she tossed them a few feet away before a massive blast hit the side they just came from.

The ship stopped as the other crew started to board the ship. They made their entry from dock eight through twelve, and everyone started to make their attack.

Captain Lush had a feeling about what was happening, which was troubling his thoughts. "SHIELD UP THIS CHAMBER AND DO NOT LET ANYONE IN!" he ordered his crew. "We're so close to the Gateway."

On the dock where Floyd and the siblings were, dust splattered as they spotted that they were caught in the firing line between the two crews who were attacking each other. They knew that this was a bad place to be, at the worst possible time.

"No, we can't be here!!!", Benny thought. "We're useless in a fight!"

There was only one option Floyd could think of to get out of a situation like this.

"Come on!" he said, as he got the siblings up, "We have to get to the top!"

They began to make their way upward, while the pirates swashed their daggers, swords, plungers, special kitchen tools and cats.

The ship was getting close to an opening portal that was peeking out. Inside it lay multiple galaxies. The ship was drifting further towards it while their invaders were pushing more the tension between them.

Floyd and the siblings ran up through an endless loop of stairs, and at every floor level they arrived, the invaders made their way and started to follow them.

"They're catching up!" Benny told his friends to hurry up as they increased their speed.

The pirate crew tried to deal with the invaders as much as they could, but the invaders seemed to overrun them.

Floyd and the siblings had to push through a few of the crew as they looked down and noticed the invaders were growing in number, which gave Floyd some real bad memories. They shortly made it to the top of the ship as the stairs led to the centre. A large iron door was shielded as few of the other crewmen tried to get it open.

"You're kidding me!" Alex yelled as he knocked countlessly on the door.

"Open the door, open the door, open the door, open the door!" Benny called out as they could hear the roaring of the invaders coming closer. They wouldn't have long till their lives would be finished.

"You got to let us in!" Lilly called out through her lungs. "We're not part of the other crew! You can't just leave us out to die!"

Lilly and Floyd began to pull the tilt of the iron door as Benny helped. They weren't sure if they were making any sort of effect, but they just had to hope it was making a difference. Then the invaders gazed over in their direction.

"There's the pilot room!" one of them said as they began to charge forward.

The pirates in the area took out their weapons as they charged towards them, even though they weren't a big number. Floyd and the others watched in horror, but suddenly the door opened slightly, and they quickly slipped in before it shut again.

As they entered the pilot room, they watched Captain Lush stirring the wheel. At the window, to their amazement, was the gateway into more galaxies.

A massively portal with countless galaxies and planets - almost what Floyd saw in his dream. The portal swirled around in a similar pattern like the galaxies.

"Wait, is that…" Alex thought.

"No, it can't be," Benny said through a jaw smack.

"It is," Floyd said, as he also couldn't believe his eyes.

"Keep them quiet and do not let them disturb me," Lush ordered as his crew made Floyd and his friends kneel down. They watched the crew trying their hardest to block the iron door - and watched Lush entering towards the portal.

"We're getting there," Lush said in amazement, "the Gateway into more galaxies."

Not only just Lush but Floyd and the Mercent Siblings admired that this was it, they were about to enter it!!!

The wonders that awaited them, the things they could witness and only could discover beyond their universe. They just couldn't wait!

But something struck them: do they really want it? With all the things they had learnt and seen on the way here. The marvellous and wonderful galaxy they belonged to; could they really leave it behind?

It felt like for the first time on their journey, there wasn't really a point to it anymore. Then as the invaders got in the chamber and were about to fight, Benny yelled out "!!!!!STOP!!!!!!!"

Everyone stopped as they looked at him. Even his siblings plus Floyd, who were entirely confused about what he had said.

"What?" Lilly asked him.

"You heard what I said!" Benny continued, "I want to get off this ship!"

"What are you talking about?" Floyd wondered as everyone including all the pirates were beyond confused.

"I...I have come to a decision," Benny spoke confidently. "I don't want to leave our galaxy, not since everything we have witnessed together. Even now I am both scared and exited to see what might happen next, I don't want to find out."

"But...but everyone hates us?" Alex told him.

"Yeah," everyone in the room agreed.

"But think about it," Benny told his brother, "Whenever life throws you a pineapple, and twists you around in a circle, do you really want to leave what we have behind? There's so much we can do! With many adventures that only the Mercent Trio can go on, and just missing what else we can do here."

Everyone looked back and forward as they weren't sure what to say. Lush came to him as he looked at the stow-aways. He had only one thing on his mind to say, "Get off my ship.

14.   We Came to a Stop

Well, not everything you expected at the end is what you wanted. Maybe that's a good thing. Possibly the main importance wasn't really the destination but the journey you made with the people you started making friends with. Maybe you came to a point on the journey where you think it's not really worth pushing yourself to the extreme.

That's why the Mercent Siblings decided to end their long adventure, deciding just to enjoy what their universe had to offer. There was so much they had discovered and never knew what it had to offer.

But every ending doesn't have a closure. On the far side of the galaxy there is a planet called Damola, a mysterious and enchanted world that has old tales about why it became that way. Union arrived at a castle that was once owned by a king but now lay in the hands of the crime boss called Earn, an eighty-year-old man who challenged anyone who doubted him and would have no one stopping his path.

Union waited for him in the hallway where the bright sun shone, reflected in the windows. Union was accompanied by three of the pirates of his crew as the old man came walking down to meet them.

Earn had small grey hair with a sharp beard and a chin, while he looked at Union with his glasses. He smiled at his bandits as he looked at three extra pirates, "Take them," he said as his bandits dragged the pirates away as they pleaded Union to save them.

After they left, Earn and Union were alone.

"So, I could tell the robbery of the La-Gold wasn't a success?" Earn asked Union with an eyebrow raised.

"There have been some problems, I'm afraid," Union replied, saying it in the most respectful way possible. Union knew that he didn't want to fail Earn; if he failed Earn, he would get into a much worse fate than the pirates. "Please, let me owe you double."

Earn glared at Union for a time and shortly added a smile. "Only this time" he said, "but I think I might have better uses for you yet, Union. But in time, I think there will be more things I'm interested than just profit."

Floyd and the siblings headed back to Osram Star to settle their journey's end as they ate some ice cream.

"Well, not something I was expecting," Alex replied. He was only focussing on just having a moment.

"Sorry guys," Benny apologised, "it's just everything was happening so fast, and I was wondering what the point was anymore?"

"It's okay, Benny," Lilly commented, "at least we saw it, right? That had to be worth something?"

"Yeah," Alex thought through his mind.

"But either way, there's a lot we can do here!" Benny told them. "They have a pool, multiple stalls, karaoke - we all can do a duet!"

"I'll have to pass on that, I'm afraid," Alex told his brother.

"And Floyd can compete in some of them."

"I'll also have to pass on that," Floyd broke the news to Benny. "There are things I do have to sort out, which I should have done long ago. I haven't been entirely truthful to you all too; I have also been running away from my responsibilities."

Floyd got up as he took out a device, he which he never expected to see again.

"Where will you be going now?" Lilly asked him.

Floyd looked back at them, "To settle some debts and some expired loans. I'll be alright", but before he went, he added, "also, thank you for letting me tag along."

They all gave a smile while Benny waved at him.

Floyd looked back at the device. It seemed so long since LO-NO gave it to him; how long has it been since he left? Time must have changed so much for him since then. He pressed a button, and a sparkly light swallowed him. The very next thing he knew, he was back in his library.

THE END

Appendix

This Appendix is included for those who are interested in how Liam became an author and how he develops his ideas. Liam hopes that this can create understanding that people with his disabilities can have great things to say and share with the world. Liam also hopes that all those who share his disabilities and want to write can hopefully benefit from learning about how he does it.

Original Outline for Gateway into Mayhem

Below is Liam's original brainstorm/outline for Gateway into Mayhem, written around 15 October 2020, which contains all major plot and character ideas.

GATEWAY INTO MAYHEM

1) We Meet you in Doom!
2) The Mercent Siblings
3) And There we have it
4) Not cording to Plan(-ish)
5) The planet of Col More
6) The Nights of Col More
7) Hitching a ride
8) Storm Winds
9) Asdorids of the Milky Sun
10) The Dead Quite Space City
11) Jolly of the Pirates
12) Into the Galaxies!
13) We came to a Close

At the End of the book, The Pirates that invaded twice in the book come to Damola (that will feature in the next book) goes to a castle use to be owned by King Nexor the Eighth, now belongs to an eighty-year-old man who slowly walked toward to the pirate.

Who was with him was Uion, the Butler. The old man had a deal that the pirates would deliver the egg, but failed, so he send them to the fire pit.

Uion promise that he'll give him a better deal to make up from his mistake. The old man take it kindly.

The Old man has a small grey staght hair, small tiny pointy beard and glasses.

"I thought you put it in a box?"

"well, it spun out of it and got out"

"huh"

"it later took a passage pod as it started to grow"

"but why are you here if you saw all of this?"

Silence, "I saw it in an operating camera"

"then I suppose you should go out there and fetch it back to me".

The small alien somehow controlled the ship with one of it's three legs as the ship crash. He and his co-polit were stranded as well, his friend was off to scout over the world, but he hasn't return, his friend think his dead and must carry his survival alone.

His verous face growl to the interduers with his swiglly mouth. He couldn't speak English, as he doesn't know what that is.

The party on the ship was going to get interputed by the missing alien, he couldn't think straight as he was trashing everything.

The crewman came and try to sunt the monster before anything gets out of hand.

"CUP CAKE!!!" it calls out.

Chapter 7 is also where they arrive at the Iceland planet.

Creatures of hood like hide in the sand storm with verous teeth (Chapter 8).

There are also drones flying in space.

When they crash landed on the jungle planet, they try to get out of the world before any monster aprouches, but later they found another ship, just before accounting creatures. (Chapter 4).

Ah! It's Floyd! Wonder what troublesome his up to this time?

The Island area is called Highlands, so it's a highland like planet that is close to the ocean.

When they reach to the cruse ship, Benny and Alex gets worried they some old friends spots them and would call secity.

"would they find us?" Alex ask.

"let's hope not" Benny said.

They turn and saw them, "oh god" they thought and looked away. They couldn't stop themselves as they keep saying oh god and try to think of a way out.

Example of Liam's unedited writing

A portion of Chapter 5 is reproduced here in Liam's words written as best as he can, before his mum edits.

5) Kailyn; Planet of the Open Sky

Lights and stars flashes through their window and the speed was so tense that no one could move a bone, or even a finger. The ship powered down as it mange to find a nearby habitable planet.

They arrive on the world of Kailyn: a blue jungle world with a pink sky as the day dimmed down by its two suns. One was still hovering as dawn was coming to an end. But by seeing the wonderful evenourment, the crew were having a problem, which Benny notice clearly, "uh ho", he said very slowly.

"what?!", Floyd asked him which altered the librarian. Benny gave a nervous look which everyone started to looked at him, until they started to hear shattering noises within the ship, "what was that?", Lilly responded.

Then Benny finally gave out, "letting you know, remember when we parked the ship back from the space station and I was going to tell the repair crew to recharge the ship to at least 86% and give them some changes which FWI: I didn't?".

The sound came loader as it was coming around in different parts of the ship. It grew more serious as the crew notice that whatever Benny did, he should've done something first before having this scenario.

"Smell that refreshing sea", Benny sighed as he tried to put his mind on something else than noticing the danger, they were in.

"why can't I smell sea?", Floyd notice.

"Because there's no sea nearby", Lilly told him, as she looked at Benny, "Benny, what did you do?".

"I totally didn't recharge it", Benny shares a guilty look.

"WHAT?!?!". The ship dropped as it was heading towards the forest. Lilly pulled it up as pink leaves dash as she tried to get the ship to hover up.

"Okay! I didn't mean for that to be so out there!", Benny commented, "I had no money...".

"we only have about less than one percent of power!!!!",
Alex snapped, "we're about to die and I am hearing
excuses right now?!?!?!".

The ship came above the trees as they noticed another
problem. A rocky wall of a cliff was coming dead ahead,
and they need to pull up in the next ten seconds.

Benny presses a button which Alex told him not to but
he did it anyway. The ship flung up as it spins to the
surface and flew through the trees which part of the
wildlife watch in confusion.

Alex looked at his brother with an astonish look, "you
press it".

"what was that?", Floyd asked as he doesn't know what
that button was meant for. Then a bright light bloom
from the back of the ship as they were diving down once
more.

They brace for their landing as the ship crashes into
some branches in lined with of few of the trees. windows
start to crack and the ship took some hit from it, but the
ship stopped as it appears to be stuck.

Alex checked if there was any power left, shamedly there wasn't as he replied to his crew, "OK, that's issue one solved".

"what's issue two?", Floyd asked cluelessly.

"we have to jump".

Liam telling his stories through cartoons

(before he could use words well enough to write)

Liam drew pictures from an early age, setting out his stories in his comic form, often divided into chapters. He was prolific in his comic-story drawing all through his childhood. Below is one example of a story.